WE WHO HUNT ALEXANDERS

JASON SANFORD

Apex Book Company

We Who Hunt Alexanders

ISBN (softcover) 978-1-955765-37-4

ISBN (epub) 978-1-955765-38-1

Cover art by Asya Yordanova

Cover design by Mikio Murikami

Edited by Jason Sizemore and Marissa van Uden

Visit us online at ApexBookCompany.com

First Edition: 2025

PRAISE FOR WE WHO HUNT ALEXANDERS

"Sanford has written a wonderfully paradoxical story: horrific yet sweet, subtle yet blunt, rageful yet loving, historical and—unfortunately—all too timely. I came away both disturbed and comforted, and I very much enjoyed it."

— JIM HINES, AUTHOR OF THE MAGIC EX LIBRIS SERIES

"By turns dark and deeply touching, *We Who Hunt Alexanders* is a tightly crafted rumination on fanaticism, monstrousness, and the power of community in a hostile world. With a fascinating new monster, a delightful supporting cast, and some epically bloody comeuppance, this is not one to miss."

— SAMANTHA MILLS, AUTHOR OF *THE WINGS UPON HER BACK*

"*We Who Hunt Alexanders* is a fast-paced novella interlaced with mystery, exploring rage, violence, and the abuse of power, while unpacking new truths and unravelling the previously known. It is a bloody yet comforting story about learning to love and trust after being taught to harden against the cruelty of the world, and the difficulty of solving problems if you can't reach the rotten roots, and only trim its branches."

— AI JIANG, NEBULA AND BRAM STOKER
AWARD-WINNING AUTHOR OF LINGHUN

"If you could rid the world of evil by eating it—by literally becoming the hell that will torture the blackguards you consume—would you? Jason Sanford's *We Who Hunt Alexanders* puts this very moral quandary before us, in a grisly, action-packed tale of murder, loyalty, and more zugzwangs. By testing the human heart under the most unimaginably difficult circumstances, Sanford delivers a

frightening, cathartic meditation on just how far we'd go for the ones we love—even when we aren't sure what love it."

— CARLOS HERNANDEZ, AUTHOR OF SAL
AND GABI FIX THE UNIVERSE

"Jason Sanford ain't playing with y'all anymore. *We Who Hunt Alexanders* lives at the intersection of cyberpunk and horror. Edginess and timeliness; blood and desperation; love and terror all woven like a rogue literary DNA strand. Sharp, relentless, achingly beautiful. Like the times we live in, *We Who Hunt Alexanders* is a harrowing tale infused with the kind of humanity that refuses to be erased."

— MAURICE BROADDUS, AUTHOR OF
UNFADEABLE AND *PIMP MY AIRSHIP*

"Amelia, the protagonist of this remarkable novella by Jason Sanford, is at once adorable and arcane, and her experiences are both deeply relatable and utterly terrifying. What I loved the most was that underneath everything, this is a story of friendship, in all its myriad forms: from the mysterious sisterhood of the rippers to the individual friendships between characters that aren't coaxed into becoming 'something more.' It's also a story about families, both biological and found. Unexpected pockets of tenderness are folded into every scene of this book about ancient man-eating monsters with entirely too many teeth."

— MIMI MONDAL, AUTHOR OF *HIS
FOOTSTEPS, THROUGH DARKNESS AND
LIGHT*

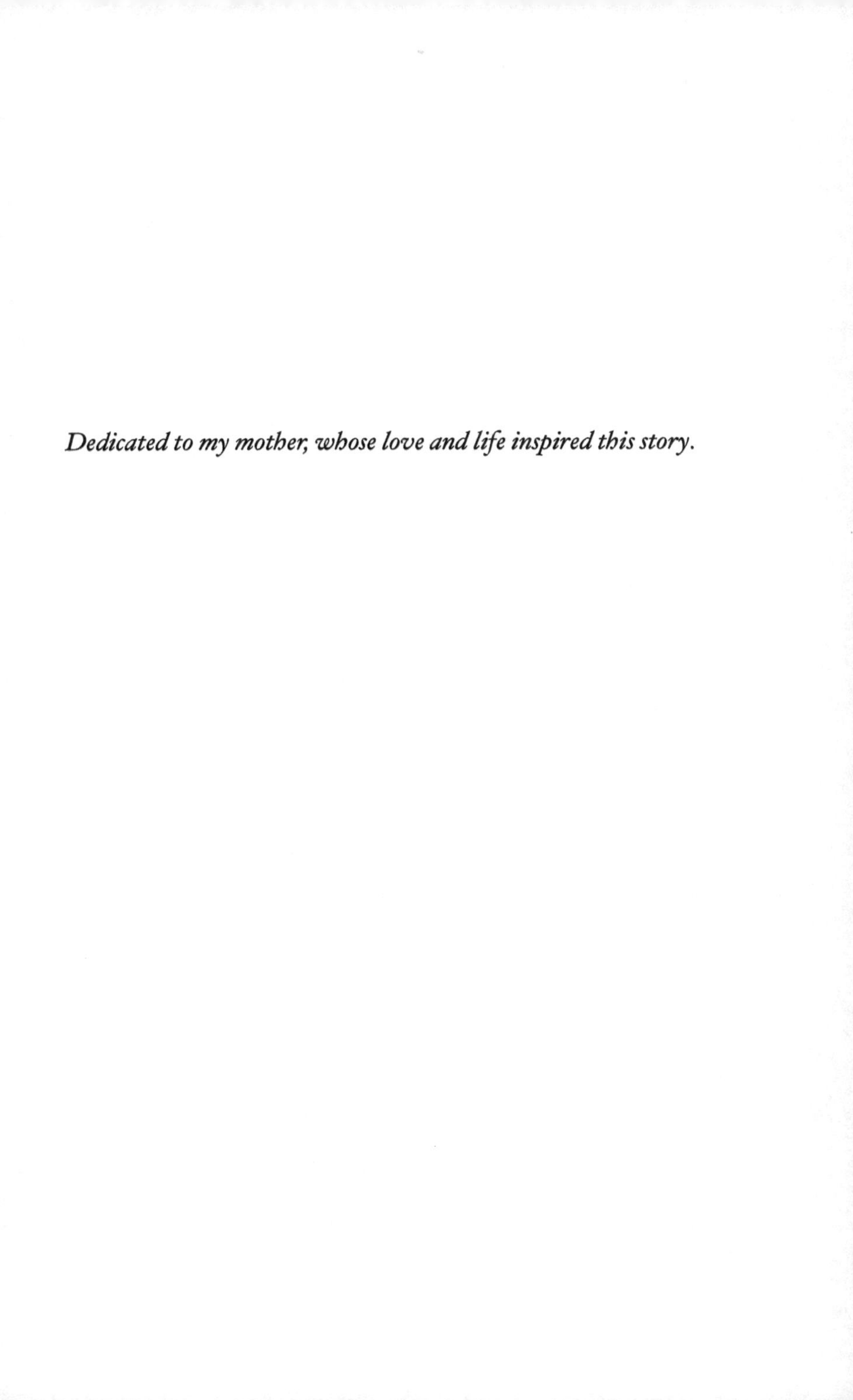

Dedicated to my mother, whose love and life inspired this story.

WE WHO HUNT ALEXANDERS

I killed my first Alexander at seventeen. That was also the age I fell in love, an emotion supposedly beyond my kind.

We rippers make our homes in the love of others. We kill the people who've so forsaken love they've burned away their souls. But actually experiencing the warmth of that strange emotion was something none of us dared achieve.

I guess Momma was right when she said I'm the strangest of monsters.

But before the love came the kill, which happened a few hours after we arrived in the city of Medea. Momma and I stumbled down the dark cobblestone streets during a howling blizzard, only occasional gaslights slashing open the night.

I hoped if anyone saw me and Momma they'd mistake us for a human woman and her teenage daughter. I also prayed—something that would have angered Momma if she'd heard me

—that we wouldn't run into any of the church zealots who'd chased us from our last home.

We passed large tenements along the train tracks with the white cross of the Vita Dei painted above many of the doorways. I'd tasted the overwhelming anger of Alexanders here and there as we fled our old home, their fury always burning into me as if I'd held my hand over a tea kettle's steam. But the city's brownstones, mansions, and tenements—especially those marked with white crosses—contained far more Alexanders than I'd ever dreamed existed.

"Be careful," Momma whispered. "There are some powerful Alexanders in this city."

I understood. You had to be careful around them. They could easily kill rippers when they outnumbered us.

"Let's go back to the countryside," I said, already hating this dirty, cold city. I shivered, nearly frozen despite the stolen coat I wore.

"Too dangerous," Momma said. "Easier for the church to track our kills in the countryside."

We turned down an alley and sheltered in an alcove between two buildings, directly across from a seedy pub. Next door to the pub was a horsecar stable, metal rails running from the building down the cobblestone street. The horses inside nickered. I smelled manure, stale hay, sour alcohol, and human sweat along with other sickly scents I didn't recognize.

"This is a good spot," Momma said. "Nasty, dark places late at night are good hunting. Remember that."

I nodded and huddled closer to Momma, trying to stay warm but careful not to embrace her. I didn't need another lecture about how rippers shouldn't hug one another.

The door to the pub opened and a drunk man stepped

out. I hoped he was an Alexander. But I didn't scent violence on him, and our magic prevented us from harming anyone who wasn't an Alexander. The man looked right through our bodies without seeing us before staggering away down the road.

This was my first time joining Momma on a hunt and despite being so cold I watched the men leaving the bar with curiosity. Not all Alexanders were men, but the vast majority were. Momma blamed society for that. She said too many men these days were given opportunities to be violent, something the church zealots encouraged.

I'd always wondered at what point a violent, angry person lost their humanity and became an Alexander. Momma had never given me a clear answer. She wouldn't even tell me why we called them Alexanders. But she did mention once that just as there are rules that govern the magic powering our lives, so too are there rules for Alexanders. Once a person bent the world too far through hate and anger and violence, all that remained for them was us.

I tasted the scent of each man leaving the bar. The men walked by themselves or in groups, some laughing and singing, others cursing or even silent. But none were Alexanders. My stomach growled, and I leaned closer to Momma's warm body.

A man slammed the pub door open. He was angry and left a bitter, metallic tang of pending violence on my tongue. An Alexander. He walked purposefully down the alley toward the shophouses facing the harbor. The evil buzzing where his soul once lived called to me, sending an excited, instinctual shiver through my body.

"Stay quiet," Momma whispered.

We slipped out of the alcove, sneaking after the man. While most people couldn't see us at night, Alexanders could. Especially when they aimed to hurt someone.

We followed him down the hill and along the street. The man staggered past rows of stone piers and wooden docks. Hundreds of sailing ships and fishing trawlers were tied up alongside the docks, bobbing in the waves. The man glanced back once, as if sensing us, but we hid in the blowing snow. He cursed and continued walking.

Momma's claws emerged from her fingers, and she spun them around, trying to conjure a blood-maw—a portal into the inner world all rippers drew our power from. But she was too weak to create a one, and I'd never been able to. She glanced at me. We'd have to do this the hard, messy way.

The man stopped before a brick shophouse. Above the door, the words DRY GOODS had been painted in gold letters on a green-stained wooden sign. The paint was faded and flaking and the store's picture window cracked, as if the building had given up caring what the world thought of it.

The man tried to open the front door, but it didn't budge. He shook the doorknob in anger. "Unlatch the door, Joanie," he yelled. "Abner, don't make me do this!" He rattled the door again.

Through the dirty window, I saw a woman in a faded robe holding a candle and a kitchen knife in the rear of the store. A young man my age stood beside her holding a wooden mallet. Even at this distance, I could see fear and determination etching their faces. Neither approached the door.

"Open it!" the man yelled again. When the people inside didn't respond, he pulled a billy club from under his coat.

Momma and I sneaked up behind him. As we neared, I

scented all of this Alexander's sins. How he beat his wife and son most days. How he'd come close to killing his wife on two occasions. I felt his family's fear and despair. How they couldn't escape and couldn't run. How his wife stayed with him for the sake of their son, and the son stayed for the sake of his mother.

The shared memories made me want to vomit, but I forced myself to stay strong like a true and proper monster.

"Hello, Alexander," my mother said as she stepped behind the man.

He jumped, turning and swinging the billy club, but Momma dodged. He tried to yell but she grabbed his throat and squeezed his vocal cords.

The man swung his billy club a second time, this time connecting with Momma's head. She released his throat and staggered back.

I grabbed the hand holding the club, stopping him from hurting her more. As he tried to shake me off, I grew claws from my fingers and two large fangs in my mouth. I bit his arm, tearing out a big chunk of meat and severing his brachial artery. He screamed but Momma grabbed his throat again, silencing him.

I swallowed the meat and licked my lips. "Hello, Alexander," I said, mimicking Momma.

"Not," he gasped. "Name's not ... Alexander ..."

"It is now," Momma said.

Momma's mouth ripped open from ear to ear, revealing a massive world of teeth. And while she'd been unable to open her blood-maw, I still heard the millions more teeth within her clicking and gnashing and begging for the Alexander and his sins. Listening to that sound was like falling from the edge of a steep, rocky canyon—and knowing that every part of the abyss below glistened with hungry, wet teeth.

She pulled the Alexander to her and ripped his throat out as he struggled and kicked. Blood splashed across the front step and froze in the frigid cold. She tore the man to pieces in a fury, swallowing one of his arms as she tore off the other and handed it to me. I dislocated my jaw, ripped my mouth into a giant opening, and swallowed it eagerly. I was so hungry.

We finished eating just in time for the front door to open. The woman and her son stood there, staring at us. When we killed a violent Alexander, their death sang out to everyone they'd ever harmed, calling them to us. Calming them. Telling them to come see that they no longer had anything to fear.

"Hello, Joanie. Hello, Abner," Momma said, touching a finger to their foreheads. "My daughter and I need shelter. May we stay in your home? We'll protect you from harm. You'll be very happy with us living here."

They both nodded from Momma's hypnotic words, and Joanie waved for us to enter. Momma staggered for a moment —in recent years, it exhausted her to use her powers like this on people's minds—and then we walked into our new home.

Joanie locked the front door behind us, then she and her son led us across the store to a stairway leading to the rooms above. As we followed, Momma manipulated their memories so they'd forget all they'd witnessed.

On the second floor, Momma and I collapsed in the living room next to the fireplace, where the banked coals of a fire glowed warmly. Dribbles of blood showed where we'd walked across the floor.

"We'll clean up the mess in the morning," Momma said to the woman whose husband she'd just killed. I liked that

Momma was always polite to people even when they wouldn't remember us.

Joanie nodded as if in a dream, a peaceful smile on her face. Abner smiled too, and they left us, closing the door gently on their way out.

I breathed deeply. The stench of the Alexander who'd terrorized this family was already dissipating. The love in this house, which had survived for years despite the Alexander, wrapped around me.

For the first time in weeks we had a true home.

EARLY THE NEXT MORNING, BEFORE THE SUN ROSE, I WIPED down all the floors and stairs and then sat next to the fireplace warming myself. Momma was still cleaning up the blood and meaty bits outside the shophouse door. When I'd last seen her, she'd been muttering in irritation as she tossed bloody chunks of snow and ice into the bay. I'd offered to help but she didn't want me outside with the sun coming up, in case someone spotted us.

Abner came sneaking down the hall and looked carefully around the living room as if a monster was about to jump him. Seeing nothing, he walked toward the kitchen—and stopped when he saw me sitting next to the fireplace.

He shook his head, as if debating my very existence, before looking again.

"Uh, hi," he said tentatively.

I held my breath, trying to force myself to turn invisible in his mind. But all I did was make myself kind of fuzzy and see-through. I cursed, walked over, and thunked his forehead, trying to rework his memories like Momma did. But it didn't work. He rubbed his head as I cursed again.

"My mother used to make me eat a piece of soap when I said words like that," he said.

"Me and Momma use those words all the time, and we never eat soap."

He considered this. "You a ghost?"

"Kinda like a ghost. Could you act like you can't see me? Momma will be mad if she finds out someone saw me. She already thinks I'm not ready to live on my own."

He smiled. "I'm Abner," he whispered.

"Amelia," I said, trying not to point out that I already knew his name. At least the magic Momma used to wipe his memories of last night seemed to be holding.

He walked to the kitchen and turned, making an extremely obvious attempt not to stare at me. I sighed. That wouldn't fool Momma. I ran after him.

"Please," I whispered. "We haven't had a home for weeks and nearly died. If Momma realizes you can see me, she'll make us leave."

"I understand. I mean, I think I do. But when can I actually see you? Without acting like I can't?"

I laughed at his confusion. "I'll tell you." I shooed him deeper into the kitchen. "Just pretend I'm not here."

"Okay. But you need to help me. If you see my father coming, warn me."

"Why?"

Abner looked away as if he really couldn't see me. For the first time I noticed the bruises on his arms and neck.

"Deal," I said, not wanting to point out that his father

would never hurt him again. I held out my hand to him. Abner shook it, and we both grinned.

I heard the sound of Momma climbing the stairs from the shop below, so I ran back to the fireplace and lay down, pretending to sleep.

FOR THE NEXT WEEK MOMMA AND I RESTED TO THE SIDE OF the fireplace on some blankets we'd borrowed from Joanie and Abner. We were always lethargic after eating—we usually wouldn't eat again for a month or so. We also slept a lot. We'd wake up if anyone approached, but most people sensed not to approach us when we were sleeping, even if we couldn't be seen.

One morning I woke well before Momma. I touched her forehead with my palm and was shocked at how cold she was. She'd been feeling ill the last year and needed her rest. I pulled her closer to the fire.

As Momma sighed in her sleep from the extra warmth, I stood and stretched ... and saw Abner across the room, sitting on the sofa reading a book. He waved.

I walked over to him. "We need to talk," I whispered.

We went down the hall to Abner's room. The walls were lined with shelves containing cheap penny dreadfuls with titles like *Spring-heeled Jack* and the *Demon Barber of Fleet Street,* along with lead toy soldiers whose uniforms were painted in a rainbow of colors. But all the toy soldiers were distorted and warped, with heads bent back and legs wrapped around their bodies like taffy.

I closed the door. "Did you see me sleeping this week?"

Abner nodded. "Saw your mother too. Both of you looked cute sleeping next to each other."

I cursed, and not only because rippers shouldn't be called cute. If he could see Momma too, I'd really messed up. I tapped his forehead again and felt his memories. But they still refused to change.

"That feels ... weird," Abner said.

"Not supposed to feel weird. Supposed to make you forget me."

"Don't worry, I haven't said anything. I want you to stay here. Mom's been happy since you arrived, and the house feels safer. Mom believes God finally answered her prayers, but I'm thinking it's you two."

"That's what we do: help people feel happy and safe wherever we live."

I looked at the penny dreadfuls again, which included a number of monster stories such as *Varney the Vampire*. Abner noticed my gaze and pulled out that booklet. The cover showed a skeleton-like vampire spreading his cape as he prepared to feast on the blood of a sleeping woman.

Abner glanced several times from the cover to me, obviously dying to ask if I was a vampire.

"That's not me," I said. "And you're not supposed to see me unless I want you to see me."

"Don't worry. My mother hasn't seen either of you. And my father hasn't been here."

He'd said it casually, but he stared at me until I awkwardly scratched my neck and looked away.

"He's not coming back, is he?" Abner asked.

I shook my head.

Abner sat cross-legged on his bed. "Good. Tell me what happened."

"We ... ate him."

Abner didn't react for several moments. He then clapped his hands and yelled, "Yes!"

I shuffled my feet, unsure how to respond.

"I kinda remember seeing something last week," Abner said. "I thought it was a dream. But it wasn't, was it?"

Shit. Momma was going to kill me. I edged toward the door.

"Wait, please," Abner said. "He used to beat me and my mother. Especially when he got drunk. Had a billy club he hit me with."

I remembered the man swinging that club at Momma.

"Did you eat all of him?" Abner asked.

"Only one of his arms. Momma ate most of him."

"He used to hold me with his left hand and beat me with his right. Which arm did you eat?"

I sighed. I felt like I was drowning, but I also hated lying. "His right."

"Good. I like that." Abner stood up and hugged me. I was so surprised I squeaked, which would have horrified Momma. Rippers weren't supposed to squeak.

"Thank you," he said.

I smiled nervously, then opened the door and walked back to Momma, who still slept by the fire. Her body had warmed up slightly, but she was still worryingly cold.

I knew I should wake Momma and tell her that Abner not only saw us, but now knew we'd killed his father. Any good ripper would immediately flee a home where her secrecy had been this compromised.

But I couldn't risk Momma getting even sicker in the winter cold if we left. So I kept silent and prayed everything would work out.

❧

WHEN I WOKE UP THE NEXT DAY, MOMMA WAS STILL sleeping, so I spent time with Abner in his room. Joanie ran the mercantile store downstairs—a store her family had run for three generations—and when Abner wasn't in school, he helped his mom. But on slow days she didn't need his assistance.

Today was a slow day. Abner and I lay on his bed and read through a stack of penny dreadfuls. He told me he borrowed them from the store whenever new ones came in.

"Do you suck blood like a vampire?" he asked. He was reading the latest installment of the *Varney the Vampire* story.

"Again, not a vampire. But there are vampires in the world. They look like this." I grew my fangs so long they stuck out from my mouth.

Abner seemed impressed by my fangs, and even more excited to learn that vampires were real. I didn't tell him that I had never actually met a vampire and only knew they existed because Momma had told me. Evidently, vampires could also turn into Alexanders, so rippers occasionally hunted them.

"Why do you have fangs if you don't suck blood?"

"Stop asking stupid questions. I told you we ate him." I dislocated my jaw and ripped open my mouth until it was large enough to swallow a piglet. "My body is also full of teeth. A whole world of teeth exists inside me. We can create blood-maws and swallow bad people whole." I paused. "Or, I'll be able to one day."

"Nice. Scary, but not too scary."

"Momma's scarier."

"Mothers always are."

We both laughed.

I really liked my new home.

MOMMA, IT TURNED OUT, ALSO LIKED OUR NEW HOME. SHE had been up and about for a few days, and appeared to be feeling better, when she told me I was now old enough to go on hunts with her.

"You need to learn this city," she said. "With this many people around, there will always be Alexanders nearby. You won't have to hunt far away like I did in our old village."

I knew that meant she wanted to stay here awhile. We'd been keeping out of the way of Abner and his mother and, true to his word, Abner acted like he couldn't see us. Even when the city constables came around asking what had happened to his father, Abner just shrugged and pretended not to know.

Momma took me out with her on a cold night, the wind off the ocean blowing a drizzle of freezing rain and sleet. Despite the cold, the horsecars still ran, pulling the cars along the twin rails embedded in the cobblestone streets. Momma and I jumped into a passing car. I stared at the miserable horses and wished I could eat the driver for taking them out in such weather.

But he wasn't an Alexander. My magic punished me for

even thinking of hurting him by burning my skin, as if the teeth inside my body were trying to ignite a fire all over me. I growled and pushed away any thought of harming the man. My body quickly healed.

We rode the streetcar until we reached midtown, where the tenements ended and magnificent brownstones and mansions rose around us. Despite their magnificence, these fancy homes reeked of Alexanders.

"You must learn where the powerful Alexanders are," Momma said. She pointed up a hill at a large mansion overlooking the street. The mansion was painted a brilliant white and looked perfectly spotless, even in the freezing drizzle. But when I reached out with my mind, I felt the darkness within. Anger and hate spilled out of the mansion, swallowing all the brilliance and riches. The darkness reached for me as if it were a monster, waiting to swallow me whole.

I gasped and turned to run, but Momma grabbed my arm, stopping me. She tapped my forehead, and her magic chased the fear and panic from my mind.

When I looked back at the mansion, it'd returned to normal.

"Don't let their emotions overwhelm you," she said. "This is why rippers don't experience the same emotions as humans. If we did, we'd be washed away by everything felt by the people around us."

I knew she said that last part for my benefit. While rippers did feel anger, the rest of humanity's emotions passed us by. Except for me. Unlike my mother and the other rippers, I tasted every emotion there was—and as I grew older, these emotions were becoming stronger. Momma saw this as a weakness, and it was probably why she'd refused to let me hunt with her until now.

I breathed deeply to calm down. Momma nodded her approval.

"I just get so upset," I said, "seeing Alexanders everywhere but not being able to stop them."

"Our hunts help people. But we can't save everyone."

That last part rang wrong in my head. Maybe we couldn't save everyone, but if I could help even a few more people, why wouldn't I?

We walked up the street away from the Alexander's mansion. As we turned a corner, we passed a priest heading towards one of Medea's basilicas. The priest stopped for a second as if sensing us and looked around before hurrying on into the cold night.

A dozen more yards up the street we passed several members of Vita Dei huddled around a small trash barrel fire in an alleyway, trying to keep warm. The zealots' white robes almost hid them in the swirling snow and I froze at the sight of them, remembering how they'd chased us out of our home village. Momma yanked my arm to keep me walking.

One of the men stared as we passed, seeing us as a human woman and teenage girl and no doubt wondering what we were doing out so late at night. He tightened his grip on his cat o' nine tails as if about to interrogate us about our sinful ways. But his fellow Vita Dei didn't want to leave the warmth of their fire, so he let us pass.

"Those bastards are everywhere in this city," Momma muttered. "Amelia, you must do better when someone notices you. Hide yourself from their minds. Run away. Attack if they're an Alexander and you think you can win. Anything but freeze in terror."

"Was that priest one of those who led the Vita Dei to our village?" I asked.

Momma glanced back at the priest walking away from us down the street. She shook her head. "He didn't smell of the same anger or self-righteousness. But we should still be careful."

Momma had been hunting Alexanders for so many centuries that she no longer saw the faces of those she hunted, only their emotions and sins.

We circled around the mansions to the rear alley where deliveries arrived and servants came and went. We passed underbutlers and footmen sheltering in the doorways of carriage houses, smoking. Shivering scullery maids emptied chamber pots and pails of garbage in the freezing rain before running back to the great houses.

I liked stalking the alley and saw why Momma had brought me here. It'd be far easier to sneak into a mansion from here than from the front.

We walked up behind the large white mansion we'd seen from the street. The anger of the Alexander living inside glared bright in my eyes. I did as Momma had said and tried to keep my emotions from being overwhelmed. Despite this, my body tensed and twitched, like a cat about to pounce on a mouse. I started to climb over the ivy-covered brick wall separating the alley from the backyard, but Momma stopped me.

"Don't make hunts more difficult than needed," she said.

I followed her to the mansion's carriage house, where she knocked on the side door. A coachman opened the door, and

Momma immediately tapped him on the forehead, causing him to stare dazed into the falling rain. We slipped past him before he came back to himself, muttering under his breath as he closed the door.

We walked quickly to the kitchen and crept unseen past the cooks and scullery maids. It wasn't hard to trick their minds because they were also trying hard not to be noticed, hanging at the back of the kitchen and talking in hushed tones. They were so deeply afraid of something in this house that their fear overwhelmed the smells of cooking food and spices.

Now that we were inside, the Alexander burned even brighter in my mind. Was this Alexander what the cooks and maids feared? I followed Momma down the hall and out of the servants' areas, into the grand dining room.

The dining room was several times larger than our current home, filled with paintings, statues, plush carpets, and fancy tables and chairs. Our old village had been overseen by a local lord with an impressive manor, but it was nothing compared to this place.

I knelt and ran my fingers through the rich carpet. Momma snatched me back upright.

"Focus," she hissed. "Powerful Alexanders like this one surround themselves with other Alexanders, who help them hurt people. So pay attention. This place is dangerous."

I nodded. On light feet, we crossed the dining room and entered the main hall. A sleeping doorman sat in a chair there, leaning back against the wall and snoring softly. Instead of slipping into the man's mind to keep him from waking, Momma gestured for me to do it.

I reached out to thunk his forehead, but Momma

grabbed my hand. Trying not to curse, I reached out my mind without touching him, a far harder way to manipulate him. The man whimpered in his sleep as I tasted the nightmare he'd been having, of a shadowy monster hiding in the mansion's coat closet who'd devour him if he opened the door. He hated the things he'd witnessed in this house but needed the job to feed his family, so he kept quiet about it, never telling anyone, not even his wife and kids.

I removed Momma and myself from his senses and pushed him deeper into sleep. I started to walk on but stopped and reached back to his nightmare. Within the dream, I placed a sword in his hand as my voice whispered that if he was too afraid to kill the monster, he could at least speak out.

Momma stared at me—she'd sensed what I'd done to his dream—but instead of chastising me for wasting time and effort, she merely walked up the stairwell.

I smiled and followed her, proud of myself.

My smile vanished as we walked down a long, dark hall. The Alexander's stench was so pungent I almost threw up.

Halfway down the hall Momma sniffed the air and growled softly. She'd never before growled around Alexanders, no matter how powerful. Instead of continuing to sneak quietly, she strode forward and slammed open the door to the main bedroom, where four figures waited.

"Greetings, my sisters," another ripper said.

She looked young, although with our kind, appearance didn't tell you our true age. She and Momma looked very similar, with the same curly black hair hanging past their shoulders, the same lean faces, and similar brown skin. But while we wore dresses, this ripper wore a man's pants and shirt.

Before the ripper stood the Alexander I'd been sensing and two lesser Alexanders, a man and a woman, who I assumed were his helpers. The main Alexander wore a nightgown as if he'd been woken from sleep, while the other two were dressed in a black suit and a matching black dress of the type worn in the city by servants. All three Alexanders stared blankly at the ripper, mesmerized.

"This was our hunt," Momma said.

The ripper smirked, or maybe she just looked like that as her mouth ripped wider. "Danjay," she said, "you're far too old and weak to be hunting a dangerous Alexander like this."

I stared in shock. I'd never heard Momma's name spoken by anyone. Was this one of Momma's friends?

"Doesn't matter what I am," Momma said. "I need to feed my daughter."

The ripper stepped towards me, while the three Alexanders remained frozen. It took massive amounts of magic to mesmerize people like that, and Momma could only do it for a few moments, like with the coachman in the carriage house. But this ripper didn't seem to care about the amount of magic she was expending.

She took my jaw in her hand and turned my face left and right, examining me as if she were a dangerous animal inspecting a new plaything. I wanted to push her away, but Momma knew me well enough that she shook her head and held her finger before her lips.

I swallowed my anger and forced a smile to my face.

"Ziee," Momma said, "this is my daughter, Amelia."

She released my face. "You hungry?" she asked.

I nodded.

Ziee stepped back to the rich Alexander and raised his arms, forming him into a frozen human cross. "Do you know why your mother brought you here?" the ripper said. "This Alexander has killed dozens of people—he has a special room in the basement where he tortures them. Mainly orphans and street kids. These two servants aid him, so they've also become Alexanders."

Ziee ripped her mouth wider and ran her tongue down the man's outstretched right arm. "When an Alexander hurts so many people, there's more power to be had when we eat them. But the hunt is also much more dangerous. So again, Danjay, I ask why you've brought your daughter here?"

Momma paced back and forth before Ziee, sizing her up as if considering whether to attack. But this ripper's magic far overpowered Momma's. I stepped forward and stood beside Momma. Maybe together we would be a match for Ziee.

Momma glanced at me and shook her head.

"We were chased from our home village by the priest leading the Vita Dei," Momma said. "We nearly died."

"An Alexander?"

"The priest? No, the priest's an incendiary."

Ziee growled softly. "I dream of eventually killing one of those."

Momma nodded in agreement.

"Still doesn't explain why you'd take on a powerful Alexander, especially in your state," Ziee said.

"I'm ... worried for Amelia. And fleeing our home increased my worry. If something happens to me, I'm not sure she'll survive. I wanted her to feed on a strong Alexander so she'd have the power to go off on her own."

Ziee stepped forward and sniffed the air, as if analyzing the scents coming off Momma. "*If something happens to you?*" she asked.

Momma hissed and swiped at Ziee with her claws, but the ripper easily jumped out of the way.

Ziee nodded. "I think I understand." She pointed at the main Alexander. "But this one is mine. I'll gift you and your daughter one of the helpers."

Momma didn't thank Ziee. Instead, her claws lit to fire as she swirled them through the air before her, conjuring a blood-maw. Even though I'd seen her do this before, I was always impressed. The blood-maw appeared slowly, floating before her body like a hazy red mirror reflecting a shivering tunnel of teeth.

A blood-maw was a tunnel to another world, a connection to a strange land of fire and rock and teeth that existed both inside each ripper yet also separate from our bodies. This world powered our magic. The more Alexanders we sent there the more powerful we grew. And each blood-maw and the world connected to it was also totally unique, used only by that individual ripper.

I'd once asked Momma how these hellish worlds within us could be separate from our bodies yet also be so intimately bound to our being that we could hear and feel our blood-maws' teeth inside us. And I also asked how using a blood-maw to swallow an Alexander and send them to this world powered our magic, the same as if we'd chugged the person down our throats.

As usual, Momma wasn't impressed with my questions and simply said not to overthink everything. "Life isn't merely strange," she'd explained to me back then. "Life exists *because* it is strange. We are what we are."

The millions of teeth in Momma's body chittered as she jumped forward. She flexed her hands as if controlling a puppet and used the blood-maw to bite off the male servant's right arm and leg for me before she swallowed the rest of him. I dislocated my jaw, ripped open my mouth, and swallowed whole the man's arm and leg.

When I looked up, Momma already looked stronger as her blood-maw fed her energy from the man it'd swallowed.

Ziee watched me for a moment then created her own blood-maw, doing so far faster than Momma. As I stared into the depths of Ziee's teeth, I felt a sense of vertigo I'd never experienced with Momma's blood-maw. It was as if the world of teeth within Ziee called to me. As if I'd never stop falling into the blood-maw she'd conjured, even as I was slowly and painfully torn to tiny pieces.

The two remaining Alexanders stepped forward and climbed into Ziee's deadly embrace. But their mesmerization wore off as her blood-maw swallowed them. They screamed when her teeth tore into them. She took her time with the rich Alexander in particular. His screams were still echoing inside her when she closed her blood-maw.

I went over to the room's wash basin and cleaned my face and hands. When I finished, I discovered Ziee standing beside me.

"What?" I snapped.

Ziee again reached for my jaw as if to examine my face, but this time I growled and swiped at her with my claws.

"She can't conjure a blood-maw, can she, Danjay?" Ziee asked.

Where Momma had gone along with Ziee's criticisms before, not wanting to risk a confrontation, this time she grew her claws out longer and growled softly, as if daring her to push the issue.

To my surprise, Ziee backed down, despite being stronger than Momma.

"I suggest you two slip out the servant's door in the kitchen," Ziee said, retracting her own claws in a show of peace. "I'll keep mesmerizing the mansion's staff since it's obvious neither of you are up to that task."

Momma said nothing as we walked back down the hall and stairs and along the alley to the main street. It took a while, but eventually a streetcar rolled by and we hopped on.

Even though we were well fed, when we sat down Momma sighed and slumped against me.

I told her to not let what Ziee said disturb her.

"I don't have human emotions, and no one is 'disturbing' me," Momma stated. "I simply don't feel well."

I wasn't so sure but wasn't fool enough to say that to Momma.

"What's an incendiary?" I asked.

"Someone who stirs up anger and hate and violence on a large scale but isn't an Alexander. They convince others to do their bidding but keep their hands clean, so convinced of their self-righteousness that they never quite turn Alexander. Incendiaries cause far more death and harm than any single Alexander ever does."

I understood. That perfectly described the priest who'd chased us from our home. He'd directed many others to do his bidding but never committed an actual violent act himself. And because that priest wasn't an Alexander, our magic prevented us from harming him. No wonder Momma and Ziee hated incendiaries.

"How do you know Ziee?" I asked. "She's not your meet-mate, is she?"

"Hell no," Momma snapped. "I've ... just known her for a while. That's all."

I was disappointed, having always wanted to know the meet-mate who'd helped Momma create me. Rippers couldn't physically mate like humans. Instead, when a ripper established a safe and loving home that lasted across many decades, another trusted ripper might be invited to visit that home and, together, use their combined magic to create a child. It didn't happen often, especially since it was difficult to create a peaceful home that was both stable for decades and near enough to Alexanders to still feed.

We rode in silence for a while until Momma grabbed my hand, which was unusual because she rarely touched me and never held my hand.

"Be careful around Ziee," Momma said. "Rippers sometimes kill each other. Especially when one of us is weak and risks being caught or endangering all our sisters."

"I'm not weak," I protested before remembering that I still couldn't create a blood-maw.

Instead of arguing, Momma released my hand, and we rode the rest of the way home without talking.

MOMMA SLEPT FOR THE NEXT THREE WEEKS, WHICH WAS strange. Normally after eating we'd sleep and lounge around for a week or so, but I'd never heard of a ripper sleeping for three solid weeks.

Momma's words to Ziee kept ringing in my head. *If something happens to me...*

Was she that ill?

I kept watch over Momma while she slept, even though there was little I could do to help. To pass the time I peeked out through the curtains at the bay and the boats tied up there. The weather was changing, and the sea wind blew to the warming scents of spring and the sweet mixing of old and new brine in the bay waters.

I also spent time with Abner. It was too dangerous to go with him to the church school he attended at the nearby cathedral. But when he worked downstairs in Joanie's store, I joined him, even though it was risky because it was easier for people to see rippers in the daylight. Still, if I wasn't hunting, it was okay—even if my powers weakened and someone saw me, all they'd notice would be a teenage girl.

One Saturday, Abner sat at the counter reading while his mother swept the floor. When she wasn't looking he waved in my direction.

"It's a slow day," Joanie told him. "You close, and I'll go upstairs and start supper."

Once his mother was gone, I sat on the stool next to Abner behind the counter. He handed me a new stack of penny dreadfuls to read, but I wasn't in the mood.

"Your mom still asleep?" he asked.

"She shouldn't be this weak after eating," I said.

"You hungry?"

"Little bit. We're supposed to eat at least every month or so, but I'll manage."

"I won't mind if you eat me."

I punched him gently in the arm. I'd already told him we couldn't eat just anyone, or even human food. Only Alexanders.

The door opened with a jangle of bells. In walked a constable—Constable Rasner, if I remembered his name correctly—and the priest who drove us out of our home village. The priest's silver-tipped cane tapped on the store's floorboards.

I ducked down behind the counter, even though they shouldn't have been able to see me. Abner glanced at me with a puzzled look, but I motioned for him not to stare at me.

"Are you young Master Andercoust?" the priest asked. "I'm Bishop Stoll."

"He's the church's demonfinder," Constable Rasner said, "and in charge of the Vita Dei."

Abner nodded. I crawled to the end of the counter and peeked around the corner. Bishop Stoll's anger and hate lit him up like a burning beacon in my mind. I now understood why rippers called people like him incendiaries.

He stood a full head and shoulders above Constable Rasner. His face was muscular, and his brown hair neatly cut.

"The good constable tells me your father went missing," Bishop Stoll said.

"He did."

Constable Rasner tapped his fingers on the counter. "Have you learned anything new about his disappearance?" he asked. "Maybe something you forgot to tell me before?"

Abner shook his head.

"I understand this might be troubling for you," the priest

said in a soothing voice. "I recently investigated a village not far from here. A couple of men vanished every so often in the countryside around that village—not enough to draw much attention, and they were never the most well-considered of men. Their families were often happy to believe the men had simply run away to seek their fortunes or other similar nonsense."

He leaned over the counter so his face was only inches from Abner's. "But they hadn't vanished or run away—they'd been killed. By a demon that shouldn't walk God's beautiful world. With His holy strength, I drove the demon from that village, but I don't know where she went. So again, I ask, is there anything more you can tell me about your father's 'disappearance'?"

"I hated him," Abner whispered.

"Excuse me?"

"I hated my father," Abner yelled. "He beat my mother and me most days, and when I went to the constables for help, they did nothing."

Constable Rasner started to protest, but the priest hushed him. "Let the boy speak," he said.

"My father is gone. I don't know where or how, and I don't care if he ever returns."

Bishop Stoll smiled. "If you remember anything different, you can find me at the cathedral's rectory. No matter what your father may have done, he's still your father. You should remember that."

He stepped quickly to the edge of the counter, next to where I was hiding, and tapped the cane's silver handhold against the wood, startling me, but I stayed quiet.

He can't see me, I thought. Please don't let him be able to

see me. Silver could make rippers visible if we weren't strong enough. And I feared I wasn't.

He tapped again, the silver tip dangerously near my body. He gave it one final loud rap before walking back toward Abner.

"You look familiar," he said, as if truly looking at Abner's face for the first time. "Do you attend the church school?"

Abner nodded. "Not like there's any other schools around here."

"Then you should have come to the priests and told us what your father was doing."

"I did. All the priests said my mother and I should submit to my father. One nice nun at school suggested I seek out the constables, but they did nothing. Probably because people around the waterfront say Constable Rasner beats his own wife."

Constable Rasner cursed and reached for Abner, but the priest stopped him.

"Yes, I remember seeing you at the school," Bishop Stoll told Abner in an irritated voice. "You're among the boys who flock around Oscar Douglas, aren't you?"

I didn't understand what Bishop Stoll was getting at, but Abner obviously did because he froze up and I smelled fear flooding his body.

"I don't know what you mean ..." Abner stammered.

While Bishop Stoll didn't have the same abilities I did, he also seemed to sense Abner's fear and smiled at it.

"Perhaps you should choose a better role model," the bishop said. "Although that won't be an issue much longer. In the end, everything comes out—just like the demon I'm hunting."

The two men walked to the door, where the bishop chuckled softly.

"I appreciate our talk, young Master Andercoust," he said on his way out.

❧

I ASKED ABNER WHO OSCAR DOUGLAS WAS AND WHAT Bishop Stoll was referring to, but Abner shook his head and didn't want to talk. He then locked himself in his room for the rest of the day.

Unsure what to do, I decided to wake Momma and tell her about the bishop's visit. Her skin felt clammy when I touched her arm, but I still shook her awake. She sat up instantly, claws growing from her fingers, ready to slash whoever was there before realizing it was just me.

"How long have I been asleep?" she asked.

"Three weeks."

Momma nodded. She listened as I explained what Bishop Stoll said. The only thing I left out was my friendship with Abner and that he could see us.

"We'll have to be careful," she said. "We must range further out in search of Alexanders—if the priest doesn't hear of any disappearances in this part of the city, maybe he'll hunt elsewhere for me."

I swallowed hard. We'd been trying to hunt nearby because going to the far parts of the city wore Momma out. But all I could do was go with her and try to help.

"Can Bishop Stoll really see us?" I asked.

"Me, yes. You, not so much. He learned to see me because I resisted him back in our village. Once a human learns to see you, it's impossible to erase yourself from their mind. You must take care that never happens."

She stared at me, and I wondered if she suspected that Abner and I were friends.

Momma didn't say anything more, instead closing her eyes as if trying to go back to sleep. But I knew she was still awake because her extended claws tapped over and over against the fireplace bricks, as if she was desperately considering who to stab to fix our problem with Bishop Stoll.

⁂

A LITTLE BEFORE MIDNIGHT, I HEARD ABNER SNEAKING down the stairs in the dark. Taking care not to wake Momma, I followed him as he slipped out of the store's back door into the alley.

I kept to the night's darkest shadows, avoiding the gaslights. My body felt stronger than ever since eating the Alexander in the mansion. I kept my claws extended and once, when Abner glanced behind him, I jumped to the second story of a tenement building and stabbed my claws into the bricks to hide myself in the shadows.

I sensed fear and nervousness and anger on Abner, but thankfully not the barest whiff of Alexander came off him.

We passed two Vita Dei vigilante patrols in white robes. In recent weeks, even more people in the city had joined them. Abner saw the first patrol in time to hide in an alley, but the second group stopped him. All of the men in the patrol smelled like Alexanders.

"What are you doing out at this ungodly hour," one of the men demanded of Abner.

"On my way to the cathedral."

The zealot smirked. "Really? You're going to church?"

One of the other men shook his short whip and pulled the leather falls tight. Another Vita Dei muttered about teaching Abner a little morality.

I thought Abner would be afraid, but instead he glared at the first zealot.

"Have I done something wrong?" he asked. "Bishop Stoll said I was to go to the cathedral anytime I needed to speak with him."

The zealot stepped back as the urine scent of fear flooded his body. "Bishop ... Stoll," he whispered. "You know Bishop Stoll?"

Abner nodded.

The zealot told his men to get going, and they walked on without another word. Abner smiled as they left. I was impressed.

Abner quickly walked a few more blocks to the city's old warehouse district along the harbor, which had fallen on hard times as more of the city's freight shifted from ships to railroads. Many of the warehouses were abandoned and the area was what Momma would call good hunting, with few gaslights and plenty of dark places for hiding. Abner had once told me how people living along the waterfront believed that monsters roamed the warehouse district. It appeared the Vita Dei believed that too, for not even they would venture into the area. One of their patrols stood guard near the district's perimeter, casting wary eyes at the dark warehouses as if monsters were waiting to rush out and devour them.

But Abner wasn't afraid. He walked quickly down the dark cobblestone streets until he arrived at an abandoned warehouse with many broken windows on the upper floors. The warehouse's giant wood sliding doors, big enough for wagons to pass through, were not only padlocked but looked like they hadn't moved in years. He circled the warehouse as if looking for something.

On the north side was another pair of giant closed doors, but one had a smaller metal door built into it. I reached out with my senses and felt several people inside, hidden behind the thick, brick walls. None of them were Alexanders. Instead, happiness and joy flowed out of the warehouse and caressed my mind. From within came the soft murmur of people talking, the delicate sounds of piano music, and the sweet scent of alcohol.

It was a bar. A hidden bar.

Abner walked up to the small metal door and knocked out a rhythmic pattern, as if giving a password. The door opened and he stepped inside ... only to be pushed right back out by a massive, muscular man.

"No kids allowed," the massive man said, shaking his head as if this was self-evident.

"I'm not a kid," Abner said. "I'm twenty-one."

"You should go to confession in the morning," the man said. "Lying's a sin." He chuckled as if this was the funniest joke he'd ever heard before closing the door.

Abner cursed, looked up and down the building, then cursed again.

He headed down a dark, brick-lined alley to the right of the bar, and I hurried after him, only to nearly run into him when I rounded the corner.

"I thought rippers were good at sneaking around," he said. "I saw you following me several blocks ago."

I started to protest, insisting that I could sneak just fine, before realizing he was teasing.

"What are you doing?" I asked.

Abner raised his finger to his lips then waved for me to follow him.

He walked alongside the warehouse searching for a side door or any other way in. There was nothing except the open windows, but they were all on the third floor. He stopped, looking dejected.

"Gonna tell me what's going on?" I asked.

Abner looked around carefully, then whispered, "I like men."

"And?"

Abner looked puzzled. "This is a secret bar for men who like men. And women who like women."

I leaned my ear against the warehouse bricks. I couldn't hear what the people inside were saying, but I could still taste their happiness.

"And?"

Abner shook his head. "Err, the church teaches that love like that's a sin. You saw those Vita Dei patrols. They whip and imprison people like us."

I clapped my hands. "I understand now," I said excitedly. "The bouncer's joke about confessing at church is funny because the church believes everyone inside is sinning."

Abner looked at me with a weird gaze. "If you must explain a joke, it's not funny." He paused. "More importantly, does this kind of bar bother you?"

"Why would it? Rippers make our homes in places where people are happy and experiencing love. This bar feels comfortable."

"Most people don't think like rippers. My friend Oscar from school lives in this warehouse. His father runs the bar."

I remembered Bishop Stoll asking Abner about someone named Oscar Douglas.

"That priest said Oscar wouldn't be a problem for much longer," Abner said. "I think he and his father are in danger. I can't wait until school to warn him."

"And this has nothing to do with also wanting to go to this bar?"

Abner blushed. He was so cute I couldn't help smiling. "The windows on the third floor are open," I said. "Grab onto my back."

Once Abner had a secure hold, I grew my claws and jumped to the second floor, stabbing my claws into the bricks. I quickly climbed to the next floor, grabbed an open window, and allowed Abner to clamber through before following him. Inside, I collapsed to the dusty wooden floor, panting but also grinning. I was stronger than I'd been when Momma and I came to this city. She'd be so proud of me.

Once I caught my breath, we began sneaking across the empty warehouse, navigating around broken wooden crates and abandoned machinery. I led Abner by the hand, because my eyes were better than his in the dark.

But as we walked around a stack of giant metal gears, each dusty gear big enough to squash me whole, panic flooded my mind. Someone was watching us! Someone dangerous—not an Alexander, but still someone who wished me harm.

"You okay?" he asked, feeling my hand tighten on his.

"Yeah," I muttered, forcing the fear out of my voice and hurrying toward a nearby stairwell.

With each step we took toward the first floor, my fear

eased. Had I gotten scared for no reason? Or had there truly been someone there?

I decided we'd leave through the bar's main door—even if that meant getting kicked out by the bouncer—instead of going back upstairs.

The bar sat in one corner of the warehouse with wooden walls built around it and lanterns hanging from pillars. There were other rooms nearby in the open spaces of the warehouse, including a small kitchen and what must be the living quarters for Oscar and his father. While the wooden walls that formed the bar reached the ceiling, the other rooms more resembled incomplete dreams of a home. The kitchen was merely a stove, an icebox, and several worn butcher tables arranged in a square in one part of the warehouse. The actual living quarters had wood-plank walls, but the walls only reached halfway to the ceiling. If I wanted to, I could easily jump over them and land on the bed and couch I saw through the open door.

A young man sat reading a book by candlelight at a large wooden table outside the bar's open doorway. He was only a bit older than Abner. While I sometimes had trouble understanding how humans appeared to each other, this young man seemed like he'd be considered handsome, with his blond hair reaching to his collar, sharp features, and a tall, lanky frame. Abner and I were still holding hands and I felt his palm turn sweaty and his heart race. So, I was right: Oscar was indeed handsome. I smiled at Abner's nervousness.

"Abner?" Oscar asked. "What are you doing here?"

Abner released my hand and sat down anxiously next to his friend. "Oscar, I need to tell you something," he said softly as he began describing what Bishop Stoll had said.

Keeping myself hidden from Oscar's mind, I stepped into the bar's entryway. Large red velvet curtains hung from each side of the door, as if this was some grand fairy portal into a magical world.

Inside, people sat talking and drinking and laughing at tables scattered around the bar. Only candlelight lit the bar, the darkness giving everyone more privacy than I'd have expected. Not long ago it'd have been difficult to keep myself hidden from so many people at once, but my powers were growing. The bartender, a middle-aged woman wearing a man's tuxedo, talked kindly with the customers. I stood next to the long, polished-oak bar, watching her serve beer and whiskey to people sitting on stools with red velvet cushions.

A hairy-faced man called out a greeting to the massive bouncer who'd closed the door on Abner earlier. The men hugged for a moment and, even in the dim light, my senses could tell that they'd both blushed and shivered slightly.

There was so much love and happiness in this place that I had to stop myself from laughing. I still did a little dance, my feet drumming up and down in excitement.

"I'm glad this place makes you happy," a deep voice said beside me.

The tall man had the same lanky body and blond hair as Oscar, but he was far older and his skin was extremely pasty white. He wore a top hat and a beautiful blue suit edged in white lace, and smelled of roses.

I stepped out of the man's way, assuming he was talking to the bartender since I'd blocked myself from everyone's minds.

To my surprise, his eyes followed me.

"Err," I stammered. "Are you talking to me?"

He smiled without opening his mouth. "Are you friends with the young man who's talking to my son?"

I nodded. Because Oscar's father had noticed me, the bartender and a few of the people sitting at the bar also started to see me. I quickly reached out with my power and reblocked myself from their minds. Thankfully, the rest of the bar was so dark that none of the other patrons noticed anything amiss.

"What do you think of my bar?" he asked.

He seemed genuinely curious and kind, which I didn't quite understand but still appreciated. However, he wasn't an Alexander, meaning he shouldn't be seeing me so easily. I glanced at Abner through the open door at the back of the bar. Oscar was listening intently as Abner shared his warning about Bishop Stoll. Because this was important to Abner, I took a deep breath to calm myself. I figured I could manage talking for a few minutes to one human who could see me.

"I like being around people when they're happy," I said. "And when they're in love. It makes me feel good."

Oscar's father bowed partway to me and tipped his top hat. "My lady, I can't tell you how pleased I am to hear your words. A barkeep's ultimate joy is the happiness of his patrons. Allow me a quick introduction. I am Fairways Douglas."

I fidgeted, smelling for the barest of moments not the splash of roses but the scent of someone at risk of turning Alexander. But then he smiled at me and again smelled merely of roses.

His smile widened, revealing long fangs. I glanced again at his pale skin, smelled again the scent of roses rising from his body. Momma had taught me years ago that these were the traits of vampires.

I edged away from him, nervously looking for some path to escape his gaze. While he wasn't an Alexander, he could still hurt me. But if I tried to hurt him back my magic would stop me.

"It's unusual to see a young ripper here," Fairways said softly. "While your kind create your nests within love and happiness, you don't experience such emotions. And those emotions are the only good reasons to come to a bar like this."

How did he know so much about rippers?

He smiled again at my shock from his words.

I stepped toward the red velvet curtains and the exit. I also considered racing through the bar to escape out the front door of the warehouse, but to do that I'd have to leave Abner.

No. I couldn't leave him. Maybe I could grab his hand and drag him after me.

But before I could take another step, a low clicking sound echoed around the vast space of the warehouse. A sound like millions of teeth clicking together. The pattern of the clicks was different from my mother's, but I'd heard it once before. At that mansion a few weeks ago.

Ziee was here.

"My understanding is that rippers don't like other rippers trespassing in their homes," Fairways said.

I nodded. Momma had taught me that early on. And now that I understood who I'd sensed upstairs, I realized I'd messed up pretty bad by coming here.

Fairways looked almost sad, as if upset at what was about to happen to me.

"Don't worry," he said. "Nothing will harm your friend. If need be, I'll personally escort him home."

For some reason I believed him, even though he was a vampire. Momma would have said I was too trusting, but I am who I am.

I again considered running through the bar and out into the street, but if I fled, I was certain Ziee would chase me down and kill me.

Momma often told me that I needed to get a handle on my emotions. While Ziee wasn't an emotion, she raised a lot of them in me and definitely needed dealing with.

Determined to do just that, I walked up to Abner and told him I was going to explore the warehouse. Oscar jumped at my words, only noticing me when I spoke. Abner stood up from his seat and asked if there was a problem, but I shook my head.

"It's all good," I lied. "Talk with your friend."

Acting braver than I felt, I hugged Abner before casually walking into the warehouse's darkness.

❧

THE FEAR RETURNED AS I WALKED UP THE WAREHOUSE stairs, each step clicking into me like the countless teeth inside Ziee. Her teeth called to me as I climbed, promising to devour me for daring to enter her home. The teeth also whispered that this was my own fault for being weak. That I was a danger to all our sisters.

At the top of the stairs, I looked across the dark third floor. Ziee stood on top of the pile of giant gears.

"Danjay will be pissed when she learns I killed you," she

announced. She was dressed in a man's shirt and pants again, although in the dark all colors were lost. And she hadn't even conjured a blood-maw, as if saying she didn't need to use her full power to kill me. Despite that, I could still hear the millions of teeth inside her clicking in anger.

"Why do you and Momma feel anger but no other emotions?" I asked. "Are all rippers like that?"

"Why would we want to feel more emotions?" Ziee asked, hopping down from the stack of giant gears and advancing toward me. "Anger is all we need—anger to punish Alexanders, anger to see that justice comes to those who deserve it. Anger at weak rippers endangering us all."

Her teeth clicked and ground against each other, the sound almost overwhelming me with fear. This was part of her power. If I'd been an Alexander, being so close to her would have mesmerized me.

But I wasn't Ziee's usual prey. I stepped to the side, circling the warehouse floor to keep a safe distance from her.

"Why didn't you leave when you realized this was my home?"

"I didn't know this was your home until the vampire downstairs told me."

Ziee stopped stalking me and rubbed her forehead, as if my statement pained her. "This is why we kill our weakest sisters," she said. "Any other ripper would have sensed this was a sister's home. And you led that young man here. A young man that damn priest is watching. Next thing you know, the priest and his damn Vita Dei will raid this place. And that will hurt not only me but also Fairways, his son, and all his staff and patrons."

I found it strange that she seemed to care about Fairways,

Oscar and the bar's staff and patrons. Obviously, the vampire knew a ripper lived here, but why would Ziee care about any of them?

I decided to let that go for now. "How did you know about Bishop Stoll?"

"I'm not a fool. I keep watch on everything in this city. Especially weak rippers like you, who might endanger me."

What the hell? My irritation pushed all fear of her from my mind, even as she began stalking me again. She followed but kept her distance, as if trying to figure out the best way to kill me without risk to herself.

As we played hunt, the clicking of her teeth grew louder, so loud it echoed throughout the warehouse. Sometimes when I made too much noise, Momma would reach out her senses and whisper in my mind to be quiet. I wondered if I could do the same to Ziee. I reached out with my powers, planning to tell her we could talk this out, but something goofed. Instead of speaking to Ziee's mind, I reached into her body and touched the massive world that existed within her.

Reaching into her felt like I'd fallen from the highest point in the sky, even though I hadn't moved from my spot on the warehouse floor. I'd always known that when Momma created a blood-maw, the world it connected to reached far deeper than could physically exist within her body. But until now I hadn't fully realized how big a ripper's world truly was.

Ziee's inner world was larger than this warehouse, maybe larger than the city. A world of mountains and valleys and cliffs and plains. And on every part of this world grew teeth, clicking and biting and tearing into Ziee's prey. I heard the screams of the rich Alexander she'd swallowed in the mansion three weeks ago, along with other Alexanders she'd eaten in recent months. She was slowly tearing them apart with her teeth, taking delicious bite after bite as she ate their anger and rage and hatred and love of violence. It was like I'd entered a portal straight to hell.

I'd previously wondered what caused an angry, violent person to fall from humanity and become an Alexander. Well, peering into Ziee's world gave me the answer. As her teeth ripped into the Alexanders, their memories played across the world within her. I saw each and every person they had hurt throughout their lifetimes. As I tasted their memories, I realized that anger and violence and hate were toxic to one's soul. That while these emotions and actions drove Alexanders to harm others, they also destroyed their own selves—perverted their souls into a horrible creation that stripped away their very humanity.

Until they became what called out to all rippers: an Alexander.

As Ziee slowly ate alive the Alexanders trapped within her, she whispered about how the people they had hurt were rejoicing at their deaths. How the Alexanders would never be mourned. How no one cried for their passing.

I'd never believed in the hell the priests spoke of, but hell was exactly what existed within the ripper standing before me. A hell personally created by Ziee just for oh-so-deserving Alexanders.

Did a similar hell live inside me?

I fell back into myself as Ziee screamed in rage. Even without asking, I realized that by extending my senses into her body, I'd broken another ripper rule.

She ran at me, fingers stretched into claws six inches long. I dodged to the right as she slashed and missed. She jumped after me, slicing at my leg and arm as I again dodged. She was faster than me, and stronger. There was no way I could defeat her in a fight.

However, as she attacked me, her skin flashed into sizzling burns and smoke rose from her cheeks—the same way my skin burned when I considered harming someone who wasn't an Alexander. Ziee wasn't just screaming in anger; her magic was tearing her body apart.

But that didn't make sense. Momma and I had both swiped our claws at Ziee in the mansion and our skin hadn't burned.

Instead of backing off because of the pain, Ziee grew more enraged. Her claws stabbed at my head. I knocked them aside, but she kicked me when I was off balance, sending me flying through the air to hit the stack of giant metal gears. The floor wobbled up and down in my eyes. I tried to stand but collapsed back against the gears.

She charged again, flames jumping from her entire face and scorching her hair, claws aimed at my face. I knew I couldn't move fast enough to save myself this time.

A blur jumped between us and grabbed Ziee, holding her back. Oscar's father.

"Let me go!" she yelled.

"Calm down," Fairways said. "You're killing yourself."

Ziee kept struggling, the flames on her skin also burning the vampire. One of her claws slashed his arm open, but he merely held her tighter, wrapping her in a hug like the kind Momma had never shared with me.

Ziee stared at the dark blood dripping from his arm for a moment before taking a deep breath and calming herself. The fire burning her flesh died away, although she still gave off a nasty, oily smoke.

"The bar will close soon," Fairways whispered in her ear. "Go clean yourself up—you smell like a burned skunk—then come down and the two of you can discuss this like good, civilized monsters."

Ziee punched Fairways hard in the stomach, causing her face to again sizzle and smoke. Then she said she'd meet us downstairs in thirty minutes.

AFTER THE PATRONS LEFT FOR THE NIGHT, I SAT AT A LARGE table in the bar with Fairways, Oscar, and Abner while the bouncer, bartender, and a couple of waiters cleaned up. Fairways said the staff already knew that he and Ziee were monsters, so there was no need for me to hide who I was either. It shocked me that so many humans knew about the two of them, and that they were all so friendly.

The huge bouncer, Billy, took a liking to me once he learned I was a ripper.

"Ziee saved me from some horrible situations when I was a kid," he whispered to me. "She's good people. Don't let her demeanor scare you."

But when Ziee came down after all the staff had left, she still looked like she wanted to cut my head off. I couldn't decide what she was angrier about: being forced to talk with me, or that Abner could also see her.

"This is why we kill weak fools like you," Ziee yelled. "Because of your actions, this human can see all rippers!"

"Ziee, perhaps that's not the best way to discuss things ..." Fairways said.

"This is between rippers," Ziee announced, the clicking of her teeth echoing across the bar. "All lesser monsters will remain quiet."

Oscar and Abner looked at me as if they absolutely wouldn't say a word. Abner nervously spun the half-empty glass of ginger beer Fairways had served him.

Fairways gestured for me to talk.

"I have questions," I said.

"So do I," Ziee replied. "Why the hell can't I attack you without catching fire?"

"That's never happened before?"

"No. I've killed several rippers over the years. Never a problem."

I frowned, the disgust on my face evident to everyone. "Those were our sisters ..."

"They were weak and let humans learn to see us," she said, gesturing at Abner to remind me of my original sin.

"What about Fairways and Oscar? Or Billy and the rest of the staff? They can see you."

"They're special cases."

"Oh, it's okay for your friends to see you, but not mine?"

Ziee's face sizzled, and I knew she was again thinking of harming me. But Fairways smirked, as if acknowledging I'd made a valid point.

"You don't like that I kill weak rippers?" Ziee asked in a low, dangerous voice.

"All that tells me is what a shit you are." There were so few of us in the world as it was, and she'd killed several of our sisters merely for not being as strong as she thought they should be.

"You should talk with your mother. Danjay has killed far more of our sisters than I ever will. Makes me wonder why she hasn't put you down herself."

I grabbed Abner's glass of ginger beer and smashed it across Ziee's face. She stared in shock, as if unable to believe I'd just done that.

"Guess I'm not weak if I can attack you without catching fire," I yelled. "Too bad you can't do the same."

She screamed and her skin flashed into flames as she tried to slash me with her claws, before Fairways restrained her once again.

❧

AFTER EVERYONE CALMED DOWN, FAIRWAYS ANNOUNCED that he, Oscar, and Abner were going to clean the rest of the bar then relax. Ziee and I were unceremoniously told to take our shit outside.

We stood in the dark just outside of the bar's metal door. Ziee brushed the ash from her burned flesh off her clothes. She no longer seemed upset—perhaps she was similar to Momma in that she could get over her anger quickly and act like she hadn't even experienced the damn emotion.

Me, I was still angry. But I was also tired and didn't want to fight anymore.

"I shouldn't have said that about your mother killing our sisters," Ziee stated in a flat voice.

"So she didn't kill other rippers like me?"

"No, Danjay has killed plenty of them over the years. But I shouldn't have told you such a personal thing about her."

Ziee said this matter-of-factly, as if stating that it was cold outside or the sun was rising.

I realized I should say something pleasant back to Ziee to smooth the tension between us. "Fairways and his son seem nice."

"They are."

"Earlier, I scented Alexander on Fairways, but the scent vanished. Why is that?"

"Fairways works hard to not turn Alexander," Ziee said. "He's careful to keep his violent possibilities in check. He drinks blood from people, but only a little at any one time so he doesn't harm them, and he always gets consent before doing so. Billy helps him out there, as do some others on the staff."

"People want to have their blood sucked?"

"You'd be amazed at what humans want to have done to them." Ziee looked at me and shook her head. "It's good Fairways intervened in our fight. If I had killed you, my magic would have burned me alive. I'm glad he stopped me."

"See, that's what pisses me off. You can have a friendship with Fairways and the people in the bar, but you want to kill me for being friends with Abner."

For a split moment Ziee's face smoked, but then she calmed herself again and nodded. "Fine. I won't kill you over Abner."

"But you might still kill me for other stuff?"

"Perhaps. Guess we'll find out together."

I sighed, which was another thing I'd never seen Momma

or Ziee do. But a limited vow not to kill me because of Abner was likely as good as I'd get from her.

"Why do you live with Fairways and Oscar?"

Ziee tapped the metal door beside us. "Fairways was turned against his will by a vampire who was a very powerful Alexander. I'd been hunting that Alexander for weeks and eventually ate him, but not in time to save Fairways. That vampire killed everyone in Fairways' family except for Oscar, who was only a baby. I think the Alexander turned Fairways into a vampire as a joke, to show him that life could always get worse."

Ziee paused. If she'd been human—or more like me—I'd have said emotions were bubbling up in her from remembering all this.

"Anyway," she said, "I realized that since Fairways didn't know how to be a vampire, he'd kill Oscar and others unless shown how to manage his needs. So, I nested within the love of his home and taught him how to survive without hurting anyone."

I sighed again. Hearing all this made it hard to stay mad at Ziee.

"I've lived with Fairways and Oscar ever since. We move to a new city or town every few years, whenever the local authorities and the church fools begin to suspect us." Ziee placed her palms on the metal door, as if feeling the love this bar generated when full of people. "Fairways likes to create places where people forbidden to express the love they feel are able to do so."

"You did good, saving them."

"I suppose," she said. "But with that priest sniffing around, we'll have to move to a new city soon."

Which brought us back to why Ziee would kill me if she could.

"Momma's ill," I said. "Is there a way to help her?"

"Rippers don't help weaker rippers."

"I don't care about that bullshit. Is there a way?"

"There's nothing to be done. Danjay is simply getting old. She's the oldest ripper I know—she's never told me her true age but based on things she's said she was born more than four thousand years ago."

I didn't know that. But if Ziee was right, that meant Momma was dying and there was nothing I could do to help her.

Tears welled up in my eyes. I wiped them as Ziee stared at me in shock.

"You are the weirdest ripper I've ever met," Ziee said.

"You sure there's nothing I can do to help Momma?"

Ziee glared at me, and her eyes and cheeks flashed with fire. "Learn to be stronger so Danjay doesn't have to take care of you. You're not a child anymore. Be a true ripper and join our sisterhood."

"And if I can't?"

"Then I swear, I will find a way to kill you before you endanger us all."

❧

ABNER AND I SAID POLITE GOODBYES TO FAIRWAYS AND Oscar, and they urged us to visit again. Ziee rolled her eyes at the invitation but finally said she'd allow me "limited" visits to her home.

Abner and I ran home, afraid that our mothers might

wake up soon. Fortunately, the few Vita Dei patrols out late were heavily into their drinks, and we easily evaded them. By the time we reached home, it was nearly dawn.

Before we entered the shophouse, Abner hugged me.

"How do you feel?" he asked.

"It's complicated. I'm getting stronger, and fighting Ziee taught me some new things. But Momma's dying, and there's not much I can do about it. How are you doing?"

"Also complicated. The guy I have a crush on is the son of a vampire. Oscar likes me but says he only wants to be friends. And my best friend is a man-eating monster who almost got killed by another man-eating monster."

I laughed. I wasn't exactly sure why Abner was sad at Oscar only wanting to be friends—wasn't it good for humans to be friends with people they were in love with? But even if I didn't understand many aspects surrounding the creation of human relationships, Abner was still my friend, and I'd support him no matter what.

"Momma and Ziee both think it's bad to feel too many emotions," I said. "They say that rippers should only feel anger and nothing more. But I don't agree with that. I'm sorry things didn't go as you wanted with Oscar, but be glad you have so many emotions to experience."

Abner considered that. "I wouldn't like feeling only anger. I prefer both of us as we are right now."

I held Abner's hand as we sneaked inside. And when I curled up next to Momma in the living room, I reached out and hugged her. She was still asleep, and I was absolutely certain she'd be horrified at receiving a hug, but I didn't care. I wanted to hug my mother, and I did.

I grew increasingly hungry over the next several weeks. Momma didn't want to risk us hunting nearby with Bishop Stoll searching for her, but when we tried hunting further away in the city, Momma's strength quickly gave out. Each time I had to carry her home.

I considered going hunting by myself, but Momma insisted I still wasn't ready. Not wanting to upset her, I stayed home and looked after her.

After two months without eating, I was so hungry that my hands shook all the time. But I didn't complain, because I knew Momma hurt even worse.

Momma usually slept, so I spent most of my time in Abner's room. I read all the penny dreadfuls I could find, hoping to see something about my kind in one of them, but even reading was hard. One night, Abner came upstairs to find me hiding under his bedsheets crying.

"Your hunger getting worse?" he asked, climbing under the sheets and hugging me.

I nodded. I'd tried eating anything I could think of—bloody meat, bread, a live chicken—but my body rejected all of it.

Abner held his forearm before my mouth. "Want to nibble?"

I smiled. Sometimes he let me gnaw on his arm to ease my hunger. I had to be careful not to bite too hard—while I couldn't eat him, my teeth could still hurt him. His trust in me by letting me do this always made me feel better.

"Mom's mad at me," he said as I gnawed tenderly. "She

caught me in the shop's water closet with a copy of the *Police Gazette*."

"By caught you mean ..."

"She screamed something about unnatural and unmanly acts. Hard to remember exactly, because she grabbed the magazine and was hitting me with it as I tried to pull up my pants."

I giggled. The *Police Gazette* was known for having very nice illustrations of men in it.

"You in trouble?" I asked.

"Not sure. She may make me confess at church. Or she may just ignore it."

I hoped she wouldn't make him confess. Joanie was extremely religious, but not in a bad way like Bishop Stoll and the Vita Dei. She was always helping other people. I'd seen her extend store credit to people struggling to feed their families, all while telling them they didn't need to pay her back. Since her store brought in barely enough for her and Abner to live on, those little acts of generosity always caught my eye.

But bringing Abner to the attention of the church would not be a good thing to do right now, not with the Vita Dei getting stronger and stronger.

I gnawed on Abner's arm again, biting a little harder. He gasped.

"I like naughty boys," I said. "They're so tasty."

We both started laughing, and kept laughing until, exhausted, we fell asleep.

I woke in the middle of the night to Momma standing over Abner's bed. She leaned directly above my face before looking at Abner, who lay behind me with his arm draped across my chest.

Momma's mouth grinned without smiling, and before her chest hovered her blood-maw, which swirled and shook as I saw her entire hell of teeth. I'd never looked so deep into the world within Momma, and it frightened me. Her grin grew wider and deeper until it ripped across her face from ear to ear, and her fingers grew into large claws.

I thought she must want to scare Abner, since our magic didn't allow us to eat or harm anyone who wasn't an Alexander. But the skin on her face and body began burning like Ziee's had a few weeks ago. She was fighting against those rules. She intended to kill Abner.

His arm around me tightened. He was awake. But he didn't scream or panic.

"Move aside, Amelia," Momma ordered as her face burned.

I shook my head, too scared to speak.

"We are not human," Momma said. "We help people. Give them peace when others refuse to even see their pain. And we kill those who become Alexanders and help bring justice to this world. But we only live because humans don't see us. If they learn to see us, we are in danger. Move aside."

I shook my head again. "He's not an Alexander. He's .... he's my friend."

Momma's giant slash of a mouth leaned over the bed, her drool dribbling on us. I was more scared than I'd ever been. Momma's magic flickered over her cheeks and arms, flames licking her skin.

"Friends?" she said with a forced, unemotional laugh. "Will you become betrothed? Or mate? Bear his children? We aren't human. You can do none of those things."

I squeezed Abner's hand tightly. "We know none of that will happen. We can only be friends. But that's enough."

Momma healed her mouth back to normal and closed her blood-maw, the countless teeth vanishing but still clicking inside her body. She leaned on the bed, supporting herself with one hand while her magic healed the burns across her body.

If her magic was healing her, that meant she'd decided not to kill Abner.

She tapped a finger against his forehead, trying to make him forget us, but he was too far gone to forget.

"I know you can see me, boy," she said. "I may not be feeling well, but if you do anything to hurt my daughter, I will come to this room while you sleep and tear you to pieces on this very bed. I don't care if my magic burns me alive—I will kill you. Am I clear?"

"Yes ma'am," he whispered.

Momma snorted and walked out of the room.

Abner and I lay in bed, not saying anything. His body shook from fear and panic. I shook too, but my fear and panic were mixed with the shocking understanding of how truly frightening my mother could be.

"You win," Abner finally said.

"Huh?"

"Your Momma catching us in bed together was way scarier than mine catching me touching myself in the water closet."

I giggled, and Abner giggled, then we rolled and laughed face down into the pillows. We then stayed awake the rest of the night, unable to sleep because of the fear that Momma might change her mind and return.

❧

ANOTHER TWO WEEKS PASSED, AND I WAS CLOSE TO starving to death.

Momma and I tried hunting one final time, but she'd been so weak she couldn't kill any of the Alexanders we tracked. She came close once with the captain of one of Medea's fishing trawlers. She'd caught the man beating one of his sailors on the docks and bit into his shoulder with her fangs. But when she tried to conjure her blood-maw to swallow him, her magic failed and she couldn't finish the kill.

Momma had told me to hide nearby and only watch, but when she couldn't finish the kill, I raced to help. The captain pulled a fishing knife from under his coat and was trying to stab Momma when I knocked him hard against one of the dock's large metal pile rings. The man fell into the shallow water before struggling to shore, where he ran screaming and bleeding into the night.

The sailor the captain had been beating looked puzzled, not able to see us and unsure what had happened. He staggered away.

I helped Momma evade the constables and the Vita Dei, who'd heard the captain's screams and come searching for the monster who'd attacked him.

When we returned home, Momma curled up in the corner and looked half dead. She was so weak that I again offered to hunt by myself.

"No," she said. "You're not ready for a solo hunt. Let me rest a bit and we'll go again."

Momma sat by the fire and stared out the room's window, which overlooked the street and harbor. I wondered if she was reliving her failed fight with the captain on the nearby docks.

My stomach growled softly but I forced it to stop, not wanting Momma to hear.

◈

THE NEXT NIGHT I MET ZIEE SEVERAL BLOCKS FROM THE shophouse. I made sure Momma was sleeping before going outside, but even if she woke up, she was too weak to stop me.

I'd sensed Ziee near the store a few times in recent weeks, no doubt checking up on me. But she'd always been careful not to approach too closely, wanting to avoid coming anywhere near Momma's home.

As I approached, she looked extremely irritated. A bit of ash smudged her shirt, and I wondered if she'd been contemplating killing me on the way over. I'd sent Ziee a note via Abner and Oscar, telling her to meet me here. She held the note before her in disgust, like it was a dead fish that had been left to rot for far too long.

"I am not some fucking monster you summon on a whim," she snapped, wadding up the note and throwing it in my face. Amusingly, even this minor violence against me caused her nose to smolder for a moment. "You better have a damn good reason for calling me here."

"Momma's not doing well. I need to get her food."

"Then go hunting. You're not a baby."

"You want me to learn to be a proper ripper, correct?" I asked. "Then help me. Teach me."

I showed her the large carpet bag I'd found in the store's storage room. I'd originally planned to go kill an Alexander, bite off the arms and legs, stuff the meat in the bag, and bring it back for Momma to eat. But if I messed up, I might lead Bishop Stoll and the Vita Dei to our home. There was so much I still didn't know about hunting Alexanders. I had to get this right, and for that I needed Ziee's help.

Ziee glared. Her cheeks smoked, and a single flame ignited on her forehead. "Rippers only teach our own daughters," she said between gritted teeth.

"Then do it for my mother. If we get her some food, she can finish teaching me herself."

We referred to all our fellow rippers as sisters, but Ziee really did look like Momma's sister. They had the same lean face and even wore their black curly hair the same way. I hadn't met any other rippers, so I didn't know if all rippers looked like they did, but either way, I was gambling that Ziee might actually like Momma a little bit and wouldn't let her starve to death. After all, she seemed to like Fairways and Oscar and the rest of the staff at the bar even though they weren't rippers.

I was betting my life on the theory that some rippers like Ziee felt more emotions than they let on.

"I'll do it," Ziee finally said. "But can that damn bag be any more conspicuous?"

I looked at the giant old bag, which was sewn together with bright red and purple pieces of carpet.

"What's wrong?" I asked innocently. "The colors will hide the blood."

Ziee's hands twitched, and her face smoldered again. I fought down a laugh—Abner and I had a bet going about how many times Ziee would want to kill me during tonight's hunt.

WE HOPPED A NEARLY EMPTY HORSECAR HEADING TOWARD the brownstones and mansions of midtown. Ziee sat on the opposite side of the car from me, near the driver, but I moved next to her once the car was in motion.

"Do you intend to annoy me all night?" she said.

"It looks less suspicious if we sit together."

Except for the driver, the only other people in the car were two women I recognized because they occasionally shopped at Joanie and Abner's store.

"Shouldn't we make ourselves invisible to everyone?" I asked. "That's what Momma and I do when we ride."

"What the hell has Danjay been teaching you?" Ziee whispered. "Why waste power when we can just appear to be human. Besides, it's awkward when people sit on you because they think a seat's empty."

I stared at Ziee. "Did you just make a joke?"

"I enjoy jokes. You won't survive for long as a ripper if you don't see the humor in this fucking world."

"Momma doesn't have a sense of humor."

"Danjay appreciates humor. She just doesn't tell anyone."

"Hell, she barely tells me anything. I don't know who her meet-mate was that helped create me, I don't know how to create a blood-maw, I don't even know why we call our prey Alexanders."

"Rippers are very private. And some of what you want to know you'll have to discover on your own. But seriously? Danjay never told you why we call them Alexanders?"

"No."

"It's because of what she did to Alexander the Great."

My heart jumped. The driver shouldn't be listening to us and the two women were in the far back of the car, but I still lowered my voice. "Did Momma ... kill Alexander the Great?"

"No, but she made him beg for death. I told you Danjay is old, but did you know she lived in the old Persian Empire's capital city of Persepolis over twenty-five hundred years ago?"

"What happened?"

"Back then, Persepolis was one of the most beautiful and richest cities in the world. At the highest point of the city, at the top of a large stone staircase that hundreds of people could climb at one time, was a palace. You entered the palace's grand hall through a giant doorway called the Gate of All Nations.

"Danjay's home was in the city's artists quarter. Even that long ago, she had no use for the rich and powerful. When she heard that Alexander was leading his army toward the city, she knew she had to stop him, because he'd kill or hurt every-one, including the poor.

"Danjay was probably the most powerful ripper in the world back then, but even she couldn't stop an army. Still, she marched straight into Alexander's camp. Rippers aren't supposed to be seen, but there's Danjay with her blood-maw swirling before her and her face ripped open to hell and back, mesmerizing and threatening anyone who comes near her and demanding to see their king.

"She planned to kill Alexander even if it meant her death, but it turned out he was one of the first incendiaries to appear among humanity. He was absolutely certain of his righteousness and divine calling but used others to enact violence. As such, he couldn't be killed by Danjay.

"But Alexander the Great doesn't know that. So Danjay bows to him and says, 'I came to kill you, oh great king. But now that I'm in your mighty presence, I'm reconsidering.'"

I laughed, imagining Momma talking like that.

"So there's Alexander," Ziee said. "He's actually thrilled at being confronted by an actual monster, because he's Alexander the Great and full of himself. The two of them threaten each other for a while, Alexander wanting to know why his soldiers shouldn't kill Danjay where she stands, Danjay countering by pointing out that she'd rip him apart before they kill her. They go back and forth until Danjay offers to leave him be if he will spare the people of the city. He can have all the gold and riches of Persepolis, but the people are not to be harmed. Alexander agrees. Danjay leaves the camp and returns home."

"That's amazing," I said.

"Yeah. Unfortunately, it didn't work. Alexander's army later swept through Persepolis and killed all the men in the city, killed or hurt most of the women, and enslaved any survivors."

"What?" This wasn't the ending I expected.

"Turns out Alexander was emboldened at surviving a face-off with an actual monster. Anyway, Danjay's pissed as only a ripper can be pissed. She still can't kill the actual Alexander the Great, but his army is composed of many individual Alexanders, and those she can kill. So, she does just that."

The claws inside Ziee's fingertips glowed slightly as she moved her hands to describe the scene to me. Her excitement made it obvious that she experienced more emotions than she let on. But I wanted to hear the rest of the story, so I didn't point out this observation.

"For the next seven years, Danjay haunts the army of Alexander the Great. Every day she kills several of his soldiers. He's trying to conquer what to him is the known world, but his soldiers are being killed by a monster when they take a shit, or sleep, or eat. And it wears the survivors down. Eventually they revolt and demand Alexander stop his endless wars and campaigning.

"He returns his army to Babylon, but Danjay keeps killing his men. So his own soldiers poison him, hoping that will call off the monster. And it's a slow and painful poison, taking Alexander twelve days to die. He's feverish and in and out of delirium. To make sure he knows why all this happened, each night Danjay visits him. While she still can't personally kill him, she makes sure that all he hears as death approaches is the constant clicking of her teeth. And that he knows his dream of building a world-spanning empire ended because of one single ripper.

"While his many heirs fought among themselves in the following decades, none attempted to replicate his constant wars, as they were all afraid a monster would haunt their armies as Danjay did. In honor of Danjay's great deeds in punishing an otherwise untouchable incendiary, rippers have called our prey Alexanders ever since."

Ziee seemed in awe of Momma. I was stunned by the story.

"Is that what really happened?" I asked. "I've read history books. I don't remember reading any of that."

"Who are you going to believe, human books or the truth as passed down across the millennia by your ripper sisters?"

"Did Momma tell that story to you?"

"Of course not," Ziee said, her awe replaced with irritation. "I wish she had. But other rippers did. Pretty impressive, huh?"

It was. As long as I could remember, Momma's powers had been relatively weak. But back in her prime, she'd been a true monster!

❧

WE RODE THE HORSECAR FOR ANOTHER FIFTEEN MINUTES IN silence. Ziee eyed the buildings and tenements we passed, looking for Alexanders, but I think she just didn't want to talk after sharing that story about Momma. Something about Danjay made Ziee both excited and moody. Which again made me wonder how they knew each other.

But before I could dig into that, the horsecar stopped and an entire squad of Vita Dei in their damn white robes climbed aboard.

The Vita Dei squad leader was a short man whose face was drawn and puckered, as if he were permanently angry. His white robes were so dingy I wondered if he ever washed them. He carried a leather whip in his right hand and had a pistol tucked into his red belt.

"And where are you two ladies going so late at night?" he asked us. "Proper young women shouldn't be out right now."

He glared at Ziee, probably wondering why she wore a man's shirt and pants.

"We're not proper women," Ziee said in a flat voice. "I'm a scullery maid, and this young fool's training under me. Although I plan to ask the master to fire her. She's spilled three chamber pots on herself this week alone."

I kept my face impassive at the insult, but the squad leader laughed.

"Tell me about it," he said, pointing at one of his men. "This asshole started threatening two men the other night, saying they were buggering each other and all that shit, how he was going to throw them on the rack until they confessed. Turns out they were constables going to work. Almost got my entire squad arrested."

"That's not fair, Belker," the man protested, "and you know—"

A glare from the squad leader shut him down.

"You're truly doing God's work, uh, Belker, was it?" Ziee asked. "But aren't the Vita Dei volunteers? Can't you just kick him off your squad?"

Belker shook his head. "Nah, the church pays us, so that high and mighty bishop makes those kinds of decisions. Damn stuck-up asshole."

"You mean Bishop Stoll? I know him. He often visits my master's house."

Belker's face seized up, and he scented of fear, no doubt wondering if Ziee would report back to Bishop Stoll what he'd said.

"Don't worry," Ziee said. "I never rat out people doing the Lord's work."

He looked relieved and thanked Ziee. They chatted a bit more as the car approached the next stop. The two women in the back of the car stood up to exit.

"Hold on there," Belker yelled at them. "We need to know where you whores have been this evening."

"They're friends of mine from church," Ziee said. "They're good, upright young ladies. Just come from volunteering with the poor down on the waterfront."

Belker nodded and waved for the women to exit.

He and Ziee chatted for another three stops, until Ziee said we had to get off. We disembarked in front of a large brownstone. Belker bid her farewell as he and his squad rode on.

I kept my emotions under wrap until the horsecar was out of hearing.

"That was amazing!" I said. "How the hell did you do that? I didn't feel you using any magic to control that asshole."

"I didn't. Words can be as powerful as magic if you know what to say. To hunt Alexanders, you must understand everything about humans. Did you scent violence on him?"

I shook my head. "One of his men might soon turn, but none of the others smelled like Alexanders."

"Exactly. The Vita Dei attracts both Alexanders and people who want to wield authority and power over others. That squad leader is one of the latter. But the problem is that posers like him can easily cross into being an Alexander if given the opportunity, and the Vita Dei sadly gives far too many people the opportunity to hurt others."

"So anyone can become an Alexander?"

"Not as I see it. Some of my sisters have said that all humans are merely one step from Alexander, but I've encountered truly good people who I'm certain would choose death before hurting others. Your Abner sometimes seems like he might become a person like that."

I thought of Abner and agreed. "You sure don't talk like Momma. She's a lot harder on humans. To her, they're either good or totally bad."

"Danjay's a very old ripper. She comes from a time when humanity was far more violent than they are today. Rippers, like every other creature in the world, must change as the world itself changes."

I smirked. "Maybe I'm one of those new rippers changing with the times."

Ziee rolled her eyes. "See, you can also make jokes. Sadly, you're not funny. But no more chit chat. It's time to hunt."

❧

WE WALKED UP AND DOWN THE STREET, LOOKING FOR Alexanders. A couple of the brownstones had a single Alexander inside, but further down the block, a large five-story building near a cathedral scented of multiple Alexanders.

"This one," Ziee said.

"I thought I'd start with something easier. Maybe a home with a single Alexander inside."

"Nonsense. You wanted to learn. Well, I'm going to teach you."

For a moment I wondered if Ziee was trying a roundabout way to get me killed, but her face wasn't smoking so I assumed I was safe.

Instead of sneaking around to the back entrance like Momma and I did at the mansion, Ziee led me up the sandstone steps to the large, ornately carved front door. She knocked softly several times until a doorman opened the door with a frown.

"Madam, do you know what time it is?" he asked.

Ziee merely thunked him in the forehead. The doorman stood there in a daze then wandered back to his quarters as if opening the door had been nothing but a dream.

"What do you sense?" Ziee asked.

"Upstairs are eight Alexanders. Two of them are very powerful, but none appears to be the leader."

"Very good. This isn't a case of a leader and helpers." Ziee tapped a bible on the table by the front door, above which on the wall hung a picture of Bishop Stoll. "Breathe deep, Amelia. Reach into their memories and lives. Feel the sins they've committed."

I did as instructed. There were fourteen people living here. Four of them, including the doorman, were servants living in their own quarters. The other ten lived in rooms upstairs. I took in their lives and sins, their anger and hatred, the pains and violence they'd inflicted on others.

"This is where Stoll's priests live," I said. "They help him run the Vita Dei."

"I thought you'd like coming here. So, what's your plan?"

"My plan?"

"I believe in learning by doing. How do we take down all these Alexanders without being killed or caught?"

"The two most powerful Alexanders live on the fifth floor. The other six are scattered between here and there. But we'll have to mesmerize all the servants, plus the two priests who aren't Alexanders, so they don't wake up."

"It'll take a lot of magic," Ziee said. "You sure you're up to it? We can always hunt somewhere easier."

Ziee was yet again making a dig at me being weak. I also knew the logical thing to do was to go somewhere safer. To find a lone Alexander to hunt.

But Bishop Stoll and the Vita Dei had chased Momma and me out of our original home. If Momma hadn't expended nearly all her energy helping us escape, maybe she wouldn't be so weak today. And Bishop Stoll had threatened Abner and Oscar. He might even come for Fairways and all the patrons who depended on him, because he'd made his bar a place where they could be themselves—a second home.

"I want these Alexanders," I said in a low voice. "No others. These."

Ziee nodded her approval.

She mesmerized all the servants in their quarters but left the two priests who weren't Alexanders to me. Those two lived on the second floor and were barely a year out of seminary. I scented the possibility of one of them turning into an Alexander, so I reached into his dreams and let him experience the pains of people being hurt by his beloved Vita Dei. I then wrapped him in a forced sleep so he couldn't easily wake up.

I did the same to the other priest to ensure he'd never be tempted by violence and hatred.

As Ziee and I climbed to the third floor, I felt tears rolling down the faces of both priests as they begged forgiveness over and over from the Vita Dei's victims.

On the third floor lived two Alexanders at opposite ends of the hall. Ziee went one way and I the other. The door to my Alexander's bedroom wasn't locked. I dropped the carpet bag before the door and eased it open slowly, reaching out with my powers to keep the Alexander asleep—only to discover him squatting over the chamber pot in his room.

"Wait a damn minute," the man muttered, thinking one of his fellow priests was opening the door.

I raced forward before he could yell or scream. The man jerked backwards, trying to stand up and pull his nightgown down. Instead, he tripped over the chamber pot and fell to the floor. I clamped my hands over his mouth and twisted his neck with all my strength until it snapped, killing him.

I looked at the carpet bag in the hallway and thought of saving some of the man for Momma, but I was starving. I tried to create a blood-maw like Momma and Ziee's, but I couldn't even hear the teeth clicking inside me. Instead, I ripped my mouth wide and bit into his arm with my fangs, tearing it off and swallowing it. I cut up the rest of his body with my claws and ate so fast I barely tasted his sins.

When I walked back into the hallway, blood and dripping entrails coated my arms and chest.

"You were noisy and messy," Ziee said. Naturally, having used her blood-maw to eat the priest, she didn't have a drop of blood on her. But even if she'd eaten an Alexander the way I had, somehow I knew she'd still stay perfectly neat and clean.

I picked up the carpet bag, and we raced up the stairs to the next floor.

I felt stronger as I killed my second priest. I used my powers to silence his mouth but keep him alive. While I still couldn't summon a blood-maw, I shared with him the pains he'd inflicted on others. As I ate his right arm, I forced him to remember the time he'd used that arm to whip a woman for showing too much skin in public. As I ate his legs, I made him experience the pain of the young men he'd tortured simply because they liked other men.

He died while I was eating his entrails. I ripped my mouth wider and swallowed the rest of him.

In the hallway, Ziee again shook her head at me. "One benefit of blood-maws is that we don't leave a bloody mess behind. Or all over us."

"How do I do that?" I asked. "I keep trying but can't open one up like you or Momma."

Ziee leaned over and held her ear to my chest. "I can't hear your teeth at all," she whispered. "Blood-maws are merely a connection to the worlds powering us. But we should still hear the teeth inside your body."

She looked puzzled but then shrugged. "We'll worry about that later. It takes too long for you to eat someone with your mouth. For the next four, I'll rip them apart. You pack parts away for your mother."

I hissed. "I want one of the powerful Alexanders."

"Yes, yes, you can have one," Ziee said like I was a petulant child.

Ziee's blood-maw swallowed the other two Alexanders on the fourth floor. She mesmerized them so they stepped neatly into her own personal hell and even muffled their screams when the blood-maw bit off their arms and legs for me, and then again when her teeth began to slowly chew them apart.

I pulled my spare clothes and the butcher's paper I'd brought out of the carpet bag, wrapped the arms and legs in the paper, and then packed the wrapped meat in the bag. I hoped it would be enough to help Momma feel a little better.

We climbed the stairs toward the final floor and the last two Alexanders: a pair of senior priests who'd been running the Vita Dei for more than a decade. I reached out with my mind and tried to mesmerize them but had no luck.

Ziee raised her finger to her lips. "They're too powerful," she whispered. "Mesmerizing won't work. Just attack."

The priests' bedrooms were next to each other. We opened the doors at the same time and rushed in.

My Alexander, a skinny, middle-aged priest in a faded nightgown, was already awake, as if knowing something was wrong downstairs. He jumped up and tried to fight me, but I slammed him back into the bed, collapsing the frame with a loud thump.

As I struggled with the man his memories flooded into me. I saw an underground chamber hidden somewhere in the city, where the Vita Dei locked up their prisoners. Dozens of people stood chained to brick walls or strapped to wooden tables. I watched the priest I struggled with move among the prisoners like a ghoul, flanked by several white-robed guards. The priest told each prisoner to confess their sins. If the prisoners didn't confess, the priest burned them with a red-hot brand until they did. If they did confess, he stabbed them with a knife in the gut, saying it was now up to God to judge whether they lived or died.

None survived. I screamed in anger at the priest's horrible deeds. I remembered how Abner's mother helped people every day in her store, even if she could barely afford to extend credit or give away food to the needy. I knew that Joanie's deeds were what religion should be, not this priest's sick actions.

I heard a muffled gunshot from Ziee's room but didn't have time to go help. Seeing my distraction, the priest rolled away from me and grabbed a knife from his nightstand, slashing my face with it. As he slashed at me again, I realized the knife he held was the same one he stabbed his prisoners with. Cursing from both the pain of my cut face and the pain from his memories, I grabbed the priest's arm and broke it. He screamed, which I silenced by slitting his throat with my claws.

As he gurgled in his own blood, I raced to the next room to see if Ziee needed help. But she was alone, save for her blood-maw. The smell of gunpowder filled the air and a derringer lay on the floor next to the bed. A gunshot wound to Ziee's shoulder was already healing. Muffled screams came from inside her personal hell as she closed her blood-maw.

"Go finish eating," she ordered. "Make it fast"

I grabbed my carpet bag and ran back into the other bedroom. The priest was still bleeding out, so I forced him to share in the pain and violence he'd inflicted on so many people by ripping his arms off and swallowing them. I then cut his legs off for Momma and placed them in the carpet bag. Maybe the legs of a powerful Alexander would be good medicine.

He was now well and dead, but I still had more of him to eat. Before I could finish, Ziee grabbed my shoulder and pulled me off his corpse.

"Get clean," she said. "We need to hurry."

I yanked my torn clothes off as Ziee filled a cup with

water from the room's wash basin and threw it over me. I quickly wiped off as much blood as I could and dressed in my clean clothes.

I was picking up the carpet bag when Ziee froze. I listened but didn't hear anything, so I reached out with my powers.

The servants and remaining priests were awake. I also sensed several members of Vita Dei entering the brownstone.

"We need to go," Ziee hissed. "Now!"

She crossed the bedroom and opened the double doors to a small balcony. Perhaps we could use our claws to climb down the bricks, although that might be too slow. However, to my surprise, Ziee leaped across the alley to the next row of brownstones. She slammed her claws into the wall and slid down in a cacophony of screeching bricks and sparks.

I'd never done anything like that, let alone while carrying a large carpet bag.

I thought Ziee was going to leave me, but she gestured for me to throw her the bag. I dropped it into her hands five stories below. She then waved for me to jump.

I hesitated, afraid. Behind me came the sounds of Vita Dei rushing up the stairs and yelling as they saw the blood trails. I recognized the voice of the Vita Dei squad leader we'd met on the horsecar earlier.

"Hurry up, you fool," Ziee yelled.

The squad leader reached the landing at the top of the stairs and shouted that someone was still in the head priest's bedroom. I stepped back, grew my claws to their maximum length, and jumped.

I barely made it to the brownstone across the alley. My claws cut too deeply into the bricks, nearly wrenching my arms from their sockets. I tried pulling them out slightly and using them to slide down gently like Ziee did, but halfway down my claws lost their grip and I dropped too fast, panicking and stabbing at the bricks over and over, trying to slow my fall. I hit the ground hard, knocking the breath out of me.

I struggled to stand until Ziee grabbed me and half carried me down the alley. Shouts and two pistol shots rang out from above, but by then we'd rounded the corner and were running down the street.

⁂

IT TOOK HOURS TO GET HOME, WITH VITA DEI PATROLS and the constables searching everywhere for us. I kept looking behind us to make sure the bag wasn't dripping a blood trail for them to follow, but the wrapping paper kept all the body fluids inside. At least that part of my plan had worked correctly.

Ziee stayed quiet the entire way home, merely pointing to indicate patrols near us or routes we should take to escape them. I figured she was furious at me for getting her into all this.

But when we reached the alley behind the shophouse, she surprised me by saying, "That went better than my first hunt against a group of powerful Alexanders. I'm almost impressed."

"Really?"

"I didn't say I *was* impressed, merely almost impressed."

I wanted to ask Ziee what had happened on that past hunt of hers, but my body ached and my claws still felt like they'd been pulled from my fingers. All I wanted was to give this food to Momma and go to sleep.

I thanked Ziee and turned to open the back door, but she stopped me.

"You can't save Danjay," she said. "We all die eventually. But that said, most rippers are killed in nasty ways by Alexanders. It'd be nice if you helped Danjay live peacefully until she dies. Take good care of her."

My eyes teared up, but unlike last time Ziee didn't get angry at a ripper crying.

"One more thing," she said. "If she refuses to eat the food you've brought because, I don't know, she's fucking Danjay, tell her I'll personally come over and shove it down her throat."

Yet again I wondered about the relationship between them. "I thought rippers didn't trespass in the other rippers' homes," I said.

"They don't. But maybe the thought of me doing that will piss her off enough to live a bit longer."

With that, she walked away down the alley, back toward her home.

❧

Ziee was correct about Momma being pissed. I'd never seen her as angry as when I told her I'd gone hunting—not even when she caught me and Abner in bed. And when she learned that Ziee had helped, and that we'd gone after six dangerous Alexanders, I thought she was going to bite my head off.

But her anger also made her hungry. She growled and

chewed me out while at the same time eating all the meat in the carpet bag.

"Two of those legs were from a pretty powerful Alexander," she said when she finished. "You killed him yourself?"

"Yes. He cut my face, but I was too strong for him."

I didn't mention how close we'd come to getting caught.

Momma wiped the blood from her mouth and looked at me, her eyes lingering on the cut across my face that was almost healed.

"Thank you, Amelia. Give me some time to get a little energy back and we'll do our own hunt."

I smiled and hugged Momma, who didn't hug me in return but also didn't pull away.

Momma pointed at the bloody carpet bag and the mess I'd made unpacking the arms and legs. "Clean that up before Abner and his mother wake," she ordered.

"Yes, ma'am."

Momma took another nap as she digested her food. I was happy to see more color in her face than before, and the teeth in her body sounded louder than I'd heard in months.

Once I finished cleaning, I woke Abner. The sun wasn't quite up, but I couldn't wait any more. I told him all about my adventure and the Alexanders I'd defeated. He was impressed and said we should go to Fairway's bar tonight to tell Oscar all that happened.

"Maybe another time," I said, thinking it probably wasn't wise to push my luck by being around Ziee twice in less than a day.

Abner looked at my cuts and scrapes and nodded as if impressed. "You're turning into an amazing monster."

I'D LONG HEARD OF THE HUMAN PHRASE 'POKING A hornet's nest,' but never understood what it meant because hornets don't scare rippers.

But after we killed those perverted priests, I understood. Bishop Stoll raged and thundered from the pulpit, visiting every cathedral, basilica, and church in the city and giving the same awful sermon about how monsters lived among us, doing unholy, evil works. And how it was up to every God-fearing citizen of Medea to reveal the monsters in our fair city. And how he would protect everyone in Medea, if they were loyal to him and the Vita Dei.

Abner and his mother were in attendance at the main cathedral when Stoll gave the first of his hateful sermons. Abner had been shocked to see his mother nodding in agreement to the bishop's words. And while the city's dignitaries in attendance such as the mayor and council members looked worried about Stoll taking so much power for himself, none said anything. They even shook hands with him at the end of the service.

He also unleashed his vigilante group like never before. The Vita Dei set up checkpoints across the city, and even though there was no law allowing the vigilantes to do this, the constables conveniently ignored them. The Vita Dei stopped anyone they considered suspicious in their eyes, such as women who wore clothes they deemed immodest or who worked inappropriate jobs. There were also rumors of even more people in the city vanishing and being taken to hidden prisons, like the one I'd seen in that evil priest's memories. Most of the people who vanished appeared to be those who went against Bishop Stoll's limited ideas on who a person could love, along with those suspected of being a monster in disguise.

Had Ziee and I had made a mistake in killing the priests? When I mentioned this to Momma, she shook her head.

"There are always incendiaries like Stoll who stir up hatred against others," she said. "I've seen this many times in my life. And he was already working toward all this. If you and Ziee hadn't killed those Alexanders, he'd have found some other excuse to do what he's doing."

"But in that priest's memories I saw how the Vita Dei torture people," I said. "Because of me, right now they're likely hurting even more people. I didn't fix anything."

I fought to keep my eyes from tearing up, but from the slight twitch of Momma's mouth I knew I'd failed. Instead of reproaching me for crying, Momma grew a long claw from her index finger and tapped me on the nose, which made me feel like I was yet again a little child being corrected by her.

"Did you only kill Alexanders?" she asked.

"Yes."

"Did those Alexanders hurt a lot of people?"

"Yes. Way more than I could count."

"Then keep doing what you're doing. No one else in this city will bring justice to those hurt by Bishop Stoll and his followers. Simply keep doing what you can to help people."

❦

MOMMA DIDN'T SAY MUCH IN THE FOLLOWING WEEKS. SHE still slept most of the time. When she was awake, she watched me and Abner.

Abner, for his part, greeted her each morning, even though she never responded to his words.

Now that my hunger was gone, I read all the penny dreadfuls I could find, although it still frustrated me that no one wrote stories about rippers. Vampires, though, plenty of vampires. Along with fairies and goblins and ghosts and all other sorts of monsters.

The next time Abner and I visited the bar, I showed several of the penny dreadfuls featuring vampires to Fairways. He was unimpressed.

"Why are vampires always presented as mysterious and sexy?" he asked, pointing at one of the cover illustrations. The art showed a vampire half hidden by shadows seducing a beautiful woman. "I'm not mysterious—I just want me and Oscar to be happy. And do you know how hard it is to find a man or a woman to love? No one ever tries to see the real me."

We had arrived a few hours before opening time, so Abner and Oscar settled at the bar to do some homework while Ziee took one of my penny dreadfuls to read.

She lounged in a booth, inspecting it, and then held up the cover, which showed a skeleton-like vampire attacking kids. "Not all vampires are mysterious and sexy," she said. "This one's horrific looking and evil."

"Absolutely unfair," Fairways said. "These portrayals are hindering my attempts at a normal life."

Ziee rolled her eyes and Oscar bit his tongue to keep from laughing. I guessed Fairways said stuff like this all the time.

"People refuse see the real you because most vampires kill people," Ziee said, tossing the dreadful back to me.

"I'm a different kind of vampire," Fairways protested.

"We'll see," she said. "I've killed four vampires in my lifetime. No doubt each of them thought the same."

I enjoyed watching them bicker. While neither would admit their feelings for the other—and Ziee would say she couldn't have any feelings except for anger—they were a good match.

Fairways wiped down the bar top and tables in preparation for opening. I could taste his worry and concern. Ever since Bishop Stoll had stepped up his campaign, fewer and fewer people risked coming to the bar. The Vita Dei even patrolled the old warehouse district, although Fairways bribed enough of their leaders that they didn't ask too many questions or look too closely at his bar.

But we all knew the bribes wouldn't protect this place for long. Fairways and Ziee had already prepared to move out quickly, which saddened me because I didn't want to lose any of the few friends I had.

Not that Ziee would count me as a friend. Still, when I told her Momma was doing a little better since eating, a smile had almost appeared on her face.

"Why aren't there any penny dreadfuls about rippers?" I asked.

"That's a good question," Fairways said. "I'm sure Ziee would feel differently about these unfair portrayals if rippers were being shown as horrible monsters preying on the innocent."

Ziee snorted. "Rippers will never be shown in these booklets."

"And why is that?" Fairways asked.

"Because unlike vampires, we're actually scary."

THE NEXT DAY, ABNER AND HIS MOTHER WERE MINDING the store. Saturdays were always busy days with people stocking up on flour, dried beans, and rice for the coming week, or with working folks using some of their limited free time to buy needed shoes or clothes for their families.

I normally stayed upstairs when the store was busy, but recently I'd grown better at hiding myself from people, so I sat in the back corner and finished reading a penny dreadful about Sweeney Todd, the demon barber of Fleet Street. Next, I started reading a story about Dick Turpin and his highway-men. As each new customer walked in, I erased myself from their eyes and ears, tricking their minds into not seeing or hearing what was actually there.

I enjoyed reading about both Sweeney Todd and Dick Turbin, finding it amusing that penny dreadfuls could also focus on humans doing bad things. I wondered if a booklet about the evils done by Bishop Stoll and his Vita Dei might change their stranglehold on the city.

My reading was interrupted when Constable Rasner, followed by five Vita Dei, entered the store. All the customers, who'd been discussing prices and which items to buy, fell quiet. One older man tried to quickly leave, only to be blocked by one of the white-robed Vita Dei, who asked him what his hurry was. I knew the old man—he lived in a home for injured and desti-tute sailors down the street. He never had enough money to live on, so Joanie gave him some food and tobacco every Saturday.

"Leave him be," Joanie snapped. "Old Barnie's never hurt anyone."

Constable Rasner nodded to the Vita Dei, and they let the old man exit the store.

"Are you really telling us what to do, Joanie," Constable Rasner said, leaning on the counter. "You behaved better when your husband was here."

I felt a surge of anger in Joanie, and Abner started to protest. Joanie quickly calmed herself and told her son to hush.

"Interesting company you keep these days, constable," Joanie said. "Has Bishop Stoll put you to work under the Vita Dei?"

Constable Rasner sputtered. "I'm in charge here. These men are merely assisting me with my investigations."

"And what are you investigating?" she asked. "My store is honest run and helps those in need. You'll find nothing illegal here."

Two of the Vita Dei whispered about women daring to talk back to men and running a store, but Joanie pretended not to hear.

Constable Rasner pointed to the rows of penny dreadfuls behind the counter. "We've come for those."

"What the hell?" Abner said. "There's nothing illegal about penny dreadfuls."

"Language, Abner," Joanie said. "But my son's correct. We're not breaking any laws by selling these booklets. They may be silly and overly dramatic, but people enjoy reading them."

"They put evil thoughts into the minds of godly men and women," Constable Rasner said. "They warp the minds of the innocent."

"My son enjoys reading them, and I can assure you he's as good a young man as you will find."

Constable Rasner started to argue but closed his mouth and waved for one of the Vita Dei to step forward. I recognized him as the squad leader from the horsecar ride—the same one who'd chased us out of the brownstone. Belker, that was his name. Where before his white robes had been a mess, now they were spotless. In addition to the whip and pistol tucked into the red belt around his waist, he also had a billy club there.

When I'd last seen him, he hadn't been an Alexander, but now he reeked of violence. I reached into his mind and almost vomited from the memories of how many people he'd hurt and killed in the last few weeks.

"I've heard you're a good, religious woman," Belker said. "Be a shame if others saw you for what you truly are."

"I'm sorry, have we met?" Joanie asked.

Instead of answering, Belker pulled the billy club from his belt and rapped it on the counter's glass display cases. Joanie froze in fear at the sight of the billy club. I wondered if she was remembering how her husband used to beat her with one. Even Abner's heart jumped. Had Constable Rasner shared that detail with Belker so he could scare them?

"We've done nothing wrong," Joanie stammered.

"Perhaps," Belker said. He tapped the billy club harder against the glass. "But mistakes happen. Things get broken. Fires get started. People get hurt."

Joanie looked at Abner and nodded, understanding the threat.

Outside, another dozen Vita Dei clustered near the windows holding large wooden staves, as if waiting for an excuse to destroy her store. She looked at the other customers in her store, many of them people she'd helped when they couldn't afford food or needed clothes for their family. None of them spoke up for her. All of them were too afraid of what the Vita Dei might do.

"Take the booklets," she said.

"Mom, you can't ..."

"Abner, go upstairs and get the ones from your room."

Abner started to argue, but she cut him off and told him to do it.

I followed him upstairs.

"This is wrong," I said as he pulled the penny dreadfuls from his shelves. "We can't let them get away with this."

"And how do we stop them? Mom's not a fool—you heard their threat. They'll burn us out or break everything in the store."

"I'll protect you," I said.

"How? You can't stop all of them."

We were still arguing when Momma walked up, telling us to be quiet because there were people downstairs who might hear. I told her what was happening. I'd expected her to agree with me about fighting this, but she said Abner was right.

"We can't fight every Alexander we encounter," she said. "Sometimes they outnumber us, sometimes they're too strong. We pick our battles. Joanie and Abner are doing the same."

I turned my head so Momma wouldn't see the tears in my eyes. Right now, I didn't need another lecture about rippers crying. Instead, I handed Abner the penny dreadfuls I'd been reading and went to my spot in the living room, so I didn't have to witness any more of this evil.

THE FOLLOWING DAY, AFTER CHURCH SERVICES, JOANIE AND Abner came straight home and stayed in the store even though it was closed on Sunday, filling the empty shelves where the booklets had been with newspapers and boxes of candy. Abner told me that Bishop Stoll planned to burn all the penny dreadfuls confiscated from across the city. The Vita Dei had piled the cheap booklets in front of the steps of the main cathedral, with the stack reaching nearly ten feet in height.

Joanie and Abner refused to watch the burning.

While Momma told me not to attend, I ignored her and went anyway. Because it was daytime, I dressed so no one would notice me as anything other than a young human woman. Ziee was right: why waste magic when you didn't have to.

Thousands of people turned out to see the burning—plenty of Vita Dei in white robes but also regular people who waited around after church services. The regular people mostly smelled like what Ziee had called posers, people just going along with the madness around them for various reasons. But, as I'd learned, it didn't take much to turn a poser into a true Alexander.

The only people I didn't see in the crowd were the people who'd enjoyed reading the penny dreadfuls. I'd watched them stop by the store over the last few months, their faces always lit up in anticipation for each week's new issue. They were schoolkids on their way home, teenagers who shared copies during downtime at apprenticeships and jobs, sailors seeking exciting tales before shipping out, and exhausted mothers and fathers in need of a break from their lives. They often chatted eagerly with Joanie and Abner about the adventures and scary horrors they'd encountered in the penny dreadfuls' easily torn pages.

None of those people were here to celebrate the burning.

Bishop Stoll stood at the top of the cathedral's limestone steps, towering above the other Vita Dei priests and leaders standing behind him. The mayor stood next to him, appearing unhappy at being there but afraid to leave. Stoll, who wore a neatly tailored black suit instead of his usual bishop's vestments, loudly tapped his silver cane on the stone stairs, bringing the crowd to silence.

"Today we purge the great city of Medea of the filth infecting our minds," he said. "In my time as your demon-finder, I've encountered many monsters. Vampires, ghosts, goblins, fairies. But the worst monsters are those who hide among us, who pretend they are the equal of good, God-fearing folks. These monsters are all around us. The sodomites and sapphic lovers. The women who steal men's work and rightful places leading our homes. The abortionists and witches who mislead women about their true place in life."

The crowd cheered.

"And here before us," he continued, "here in this pile of rotting sin, are the fruits of these monsters. These booklets pervert the minds of this city's innocents with filthy stories and lies. These booklets allow the monsters to prey upon us. But no more!"

Bishop Stoll spoke with anger and hatred, and the crowd responded to each word, amplifying and feeding off his emotions. While he hadn't done any violence himself, hadn't actually crossed the line into becoming an Alexander, I knew his words would turn many of these people. They'd take what he said and go out and hurt others. They'd kill those they hated. Far too many in this crowd were all too eager—even willing—to become Alexanders.

Bishop Stoll was indeed an incendiary, as Momma had declared.

Belker stepped forward in his white robes and tossed a burning torch into the pile of penny dreadfuls. The booklets ignited quickly, the pile screaming into a blazing fire and pulling the air around us towards itself.

People screamed louder than the fire and began pushing each other in excitement, trying to throw additional penny dreadfuls into the blaze. I edged away as white robed Vita Dei danced up and down, shouting Bishop Stoll's name.

Two Vita Dei saw me leaving and asked where I was going, but I ran past them toward the waterfront and home.

I realized it was only a matter of time before this city exploded into violence. All because of Bishop Stoll.

And since he wasn't an Alexander, there was no way for me, Momma, or Ziee to stop him.

❧

THE FOLLOWING NIGHT, MOMMA AND I WENT FOR another hunt. While she'd gained more strength and was feeling better than she had in months, she was still not as powerful as she'd been before we'd fled our village.

But when I'd told Momma what I witnessed at Bishop Stoll's burning, a fire jumped into her eyes I hadn't seen since we'd fled our old home. I could taste her anger at what Stoll had instigated.

"In dangerous times, sometimes all rippers can do to help is hunt," she announced. "If we give even one person justice, it's worth the risk."

But her lofty words didn't make up for her weak body. Because of this, we took care about which Alexanders we targeted. Around midnight we followed a group of Vita Dei at a distance, all of whom were Alexanders. The group had already attacked several teenagers they caught drinking along the docks, with the Vita Dei clubbing the young men and women before forcing them to kneel on the cobblestones and beg forgiveness.

Thankfully the Vita Dei didn't kill the teenagers, being satisfied with merely hurting them. The Vita Dei then marched onward in search of other victims. Momma and I followed them at a distance, hoping they'd separate so we could grab one without the others noticing.

"I blame myself," Momma whispered. "Maybe if I'd done something differently, I could have stopped this before it began."

"It's not your fault," I said. "You were right—there were too many Vita Dei in the store. We couldn't have stopped them without Joanie and Abner getting hurt."

"That's not what I mean. I blame myself for Bishop Stole getting so popular. If I'd stopped him in our village, he'd have never come here and gained all this power."

I agreed, but wasn't sure how we could have stopped him since he wasn't an Alexander. I remembered Momma fighting him and his Vita Dei back when they found us in our village. They'd caught us by surprise, threatening to kill the family we lived with unless Momma surrendered. Because they didn't see or know about me, Momma told me to sneak away and she'd catch up. But instead of fleeing, I hid behind the neighbor's house and watched as Momma stepped from our home with her hands raised. Bishop Stoll allowed the family we'd lived with to escape but they attacked Momma with rifles and pistols. She killed two of the Vita Dei but the others, including Stoll, weren't Alexanders. Every time she tried to attack Stoll and the others her body erupted in flames. They nearly caught her, shooting her several times, but at the last minute she saw an opening and bolted for the river. I ran after her and, when she stumbled and collapsed from the gunshot wounds and flames, I picked her up. We jumped into the river, letting the current carry us away. The magic flames that burned her skin for daring to fight people who weren't Alexanders also burned me when I grabbed her, but I hadn't complained because I knew how hard she'd fought to save us.

"You did all you could," I said. "I was so proud of you that day."

Momma nodded. If she was pleased with my words, she didn't say. Instead, she pointed to the group of Vita Dei we'd been tailing. One of the men was walking to a still-open bar down the block, possibly to pick up beers or food for his squad. We raced down the street and into a side alley, where we waited for him. As he walked by, I grabbed him and pulled him into the alley, keeping my hands over his mouth so he couldn't scream. Momma tried opening a blood-maw, swirling her fingers before her, but the first two attempts flicked out. Her blood-maws were taking longer than ever to create. Finally, on the third attempt, she succeeded. I ripped off one of the Alexander's legs as Momma swallowed him.

Momma's blood-maw vanished, leaving only the sound of chittering teeth and the muffled screams of the man receiving his just punishment. While he was only a recently turned Alexander, he'd still hurt many people.

We sneaked back toward home as dawn approached, but our path along the waterfront was blocked by a dozen Vita Dei, so we climbed to the roof of a shophouse to wait for them to move.

As we sat there, I looked out over the harbor. Despite all we'd been through, I now liked this city.

I noticed Momma staring at me.

"What?" I asked.

"I heard the teeth within you for a moment. Back when we grabbed that Alexander."

I smiled. "Really? Will I be able to open a blood-maw soon?"

"I don't know. Most rippers are much younger than you when they create their first blood-maws."

I held my hand to my chest. Not only had I never heard the teeth within me, I'd never felt my connected world either.

"What if I don't have a world within me?" I asked.

"You do. You couldn't use your other powers without it. Perhaps your world is still developing. The worlds within us develop from the anger we feel at injustice and evil, and each world differs based on the type of ripper who created it."

I remembered Ziee talking about how many "weak" rippers Momma had killed during her lifetime.

"Momma," I said in a low voice. "Why didn't you kill me?"

"What?" She almost seemed shocked.

"Ziee told me you've killed plenty of rippers over the years because they were weak. Rippers like me."

I tasted anger in Momma, the only emotion she ever felt. I wondered if she was thinking about killing Ziee.

"That's how my mother raised me, and her mother her," Momma said. "This was thousands of years ago. Back then, you could kill a few Alexanders and bring peace to an area for decades. But then the world changed. Instead of a few Alexanders, rippers began to face armies of them. And incendiaries who couldn't be touched."

She looked down at the group of Vita Dei blocking our way home. Only a few of them were Alexanders, but still too many for us to sneak past.

"Now we could kill an Alexander every single day and the people of this city still wouldn't be safe. Not when incendiaries like Bishop Stoll infect so many others with hate and anger and violence. Despite that, we have to keep trying."

Momma growled as she again looked at the Vita Dei below us. Was Momma remembering the time she faced off against Alexander the Great and his army? Did she see Bishop Stoll as one of his incendiary heirs?

"Ziee is correct. I have killed many rippers over the years. Now I wonder if I was wrong. When I birthed you, I realized I didn't have much time left. You're my last daughter, and I've tried hard not to infect you with the many mistakes I've made in my life. All I can say is, do better than I have done."

I shivered. I wanted to hug her, but I also didn't want to break this moment. She'd never before revealed so much of herself to me.

"Don't be angry at Ziee for telling me," I said.

Momma sighed. It was the first time I'd ever heard her actually sigh—I hadn't known she could even do that.

"I can't stay mad at Ziee," Momma said. "She's my only living grandchild."

"What!"

"Her mother—your older sister— was killed by Alexanders centuries ago when Ziee was still a child. I raised Ziee until she could survive on her own.'"

That explained so much. I wanted to ask why they'd never told me, but I also knew this was how rippers always behaved. They protected their young but, once we grew up, we were on our own. That and the whole "rippers don't experience emotions" bullshit.

I grinned as a delicious thought entered my mind. If Ziee's mother was my older sister, that made me her aunt.

"I imagine it'll really piss off Ziee if I told her to call me Auntie Amelia," I said.

Momma almost smiled. "It will indeed. Tell her I said to call you that."

❧

EVENTUALLY THE VITA DEI BLOCKING US FROM THE shophouse wandered off and me and Momma reached home. Despite eating, Momma was exhausted and slept for the rest of the week. During that time, I tried hunting by myself but without success. Unfortunately, the Vita Dei squads seemed even more paranoid than usual, so I didn't have a chance to catch one of them wandering off by himself.

Then Sunday arrived. Joanie and Abner went to church, as usual. During one of my hunts I'd found an old, ragged penny dreadful thrown away in an alley, so I sat reading it next to Momma, who still slept by the fireplace. I growled when I discovered that the booklet's best story, about a corrupt and nasty aristocrat haunted by the ghost of a spurned lover, was missing the final three pages.

I was trying to calm my anger when I heard the door downstairs bang shut and Abner run up the stairs.

"He's coming," Abner yelled. "Bishop Stoll will soon be here."

"What do you mean?" Momma snapped, irritated at being woken up.

"My mother invited him for Sunday dinner," he said. "Since Mom caught me in the water closet, and since the Vita Dei threatened us, she's been talking with him and his assistants. I think she's trying to protect us by being nice to him."

Momma glanced at me with a puzzled look, no doubt wanting to know what had happened in the water closet, but I shook my head. Now wasn't the time to explain.

"Maybe he's just coming to eat," I said.

"No, he asked again about my father. I think he knows you're here."

Momma growled. She waved for me and Abner to sit on the sofa.

"Are you truly willing to help my daughter?" she asked Abner.

He nodded.

"Amelia is my ninth daughter," Momma said softly. "While some of my daughters lived long lives, I still witnessed all their deaths. This world eventually kills every ripper. That's because of what we are, because we feed only on dangerous people who have so abandoned love they've destroyed their souls."

I didn't know that Momma had lost so many daughters

before me. That explained why she'd fought so hard against me hunting alone.

"I'm dying," Momma said. "Maybe another year if I eat. Less if I don't. Either way, death will claim me."

I looked away, not wanting to think about Momma being taken from me. I knew this was coming, but ...

Abner hugged me, causing Momma to raise an eyebrow.

"Again, do you truly want to help my daughter?" Momma asked. Her mouth grew larger until her grin ran from ear to ear.

Abner shivered in fear. But he also nodded.

BISHOP STOLL SHOWED UP FOR SUNDAY DINNER LATER IN the afternoon. Joanie had spent the last few hours cooking, with Abner helping out. Once the priest knocked on the main door downstairs, Momma and I slipped out the back.

It was strange to walk around town during the daytime when we were easier to see. People glanced at us but then looked away, seeing us as simply a mother and daughter out for a Sunday afternoon walk. But when we passed an Alexander and they began to recognize us as dangerous, Momma was forced to slip into their minds to make them forget us. I could tell the effort drained her.

We walked down to the harbor. Most of Medea's fishing vessels were in port for the day while larger sailing ships were loading and unloading cargo. The more well-off families walked along the docks in their Sunday best—gentlemen in waistcoats and top hats, ladies in petticoats and calico skirts and bonnets. Poorer families came in whatever decent clothes they owned. And everywhere kids ran around squealing or begging their parents for shaved ice and other sweets.

"This isn't as fancy as the parks in the rich parts of town, but I think it's nicer," Momma said.

The happiness of the people washed over us. I had never been around so many people at once during the daytime. I stumbled from feeling so many emotions at once. Momma held my shoulder to steady me.

"Remember that most people are good," she whispered. "Often ignorant, yes. Willing to overlook wrongs, yes. Yet still good."

I smiled.

After a few hours, Momma was exhausted. We figured Bishop Stoll would have finished Sunday dinner and left, so we walked back home. However, as we neared the shop's front door, it opened to reveal Constable Rasner stepping out. I felt the anger and violence in the man and knew he was now fully an Alexander.

"Are you not feeling well, ma'am?" he asked in a tone far more polite than the emotions swirling inside him. He looked straight at Momma, who leaned on me for support. He also looked me over, with the daylight stopping me from hiding myself from his eyes.

Momma tried reaching out with her mind, but he was a powerful Alexander who had seen her, and she was too weak.

"Momma had a little too much sun," I said as we continued walking on past him.

Constable Rasner tipped his bobby hat backwards, looking at us with curious eyes. "I can call some of my men, if you need help."

As he said that, I tasted more Alexanders surrounding the

shophouse: three of them back in the alley near the rear door to the store, two others around the corner. All members of the Vita Dei.

"We'll be fine," I said. "We're going to catch the horsecar and take it home."

I walked faster, almost dragging Momma with me. I didn't look back, but I didn't need to—I felt Constable Rasner walking after us.

"Strange," he said. "I've never seen either of you around here."

My stomach growled as he followed us down the cobblestone street. For the first time, I felt and heard the millions of teeth within my body grinding against each other. The claws inside my fingers burned. Being so near an Alexander—and having him threaten Momma—was opening myself to more power than I'd ever known. I bit my lower lip, straining against my magic and the need to punish this Alexander.

One of the constable's men—also an Alexander—stood just down the street, leaning half-hidden inside the entryway to another shophouse. I felt myself losing control. But if I did, everyone would see, not only the constables and Vita Dei but also the regular people walking up and down the street.

"Wait, you," Constable Rasner yelled as he grabbed my shoulder, stopping me.

I turned and looked at him but couldn't say anything, barely keeping control of myself.

He pulled out a small notebook. "I need your names," he said. "And where you live."

I tasted his memories of the countless times he'd beat his wife and kids. Of the many people he'd deliberately hurt over the years in his job. Of the people he's killed recently as he worked alongside the Vita Dei. Of his perverse enjoyment of violence.

I needed to eat him. I wanted to swallow him whole. The world would be a better place without him. I fought so hard against my body, I started shaking.

"What's wrong with you, girl?" he asked.

I felt my fangs growing and my mouth threatening to rip into a massive, scary grin. Just as I was about to attack him, Momma's strong hand rested on my shoulder, both calming and restraining me.

"My apologies, constable," she said. "My daughter gets nervous around the police. She tries ever so hard to be a good girl."

Constable Rasner straightened his bobby hat. "Understandable, ma'am. Now where do you live?"

"In the tenements on Asgor Street, the last stop before the horsecars reach midtown. We were visiting friends today."

As Momma spoke, I felt her words wrapping around Constable Rasner's mind, convincing him of the truth of what she'd said.

"I don't know," Constable Rasner said, resisting. "Bishop Stoll has us looking for a suspicious woman living around here. But she's not really a woman. More like a monster."

"Just one woman?" Momma asked. "Or a mother and daughter?"

As Momma's power pushed through Constable Rasner's mind, he smiled. "Good point. No way the woman we want is a mother like yourself. Do you need help reaching the horsecar stop?"

Momma straightened herself up with a strength she

shouldn't have had. "Thank you, but no. I'm feeling much better."

We walked on, turned the corner, and walked up another street, passing the alley with the seedy bar where we'd stalked Joanie's husband that first night in Medea. The next street up, we stopped at the horsecar stop.

But one of Constable Rasner's men had still followed us all the way here. As we waited for the next streetcar, I felt the Alexander watching us. Momma squeezed my hand. When the streetcar stopped and we climbed on, we sat near the back. I saw that the Alexander was still staring at us.

"Wave at him," Momma said. "Pretend you're a young lady being polite."

I did as told. Once the streetcar pulled away and we were out of sight, Momma collapsed in her seat.

"He's smart," Momma whispered.

"Who?"

"Bishop Stoll. He knows that being out in the daytime forces me to use my powers, weakening me. He probably figured I'd attack one of the constables or try to force my way back into the house."

"But he didn't know about me."

"No, he didn't know about my daughter. Being together saved us."

I hugged Momma tight, despite her views on hugs being something rippers didn't do.

"I love you," I said.

"Truly?" she asked.

I blushed and looked down. Rippers weren't supposed to experience love. We live surrounded by it, yes, but weren't supposed to experience it.

Despite that, I knew I did. I'd felt the emotion building in me for years. More so since moving to this city.

"I do," I whispered. "I love you."

Momma looked at me with a puzzled gaze. "What's it like, to experience love?"

I thought for a moment. "Love is so many things all at once," I said. "Love is wanting to be with someone. Wanting to hug them and never let go. Love is happiness. Love is feeling protected and being protective. Love is the whole world embracing you and the one you love."

Momma nodded solemnly. "Hmm, does that mean I love you because I protect you?"

I wanted to say yes, but I also knew Momma protected me out of ripper instinct, not love. She'd give her life for me, but that's what rippers did for their children. She'd never known love and likely never would.

"No," I said, "I wish you did. But I know that's not what you feel."

Momma squirmed from being hugged and I let her go, sad that she didn't feel the things I did and that I couldn't explain better what love felt like.

Momma patted my head, the closest she'd ever come to showing affection for me. "You've always been a strange one," she said, "but there's no wrong in that. I'm glad you're my daughter."

I smiled, pretending her words were Momma's way of saying "I love you, too."

WE RODE THE STREETCAR IN LOOPS UNTIL LATE AT NIGHT, when we switched to a new one. And then we rode even more.

By the time we returned home, Momma was barely conscious. She leaned her full weight on me and staggered alongside my feet. I easily supported her as I felt my body growing stronger, as if the power that had nearly forced me to attack Constable Rasner was now directed toward helping us reach home.

The Vita Dei still surrounded the shophouse, but Constable Rasner and his men had left. I sensed that one of these Vita Dei had the potential to be an Alexander, but none were right now.

They shouldn't have noticed us walking by, but I still reached out with my mind and blocked us from their senses to make sure. We slipped through the back door.

Abner sat in the dark at the bottom of the stairs.

"What happened?" he asked as he took one of Momma's arms. Together, we carried her up the stairs. "I searched all over for you."

I shook my head, not able to answer right now. I started to move Momma toward the warmth of the fireplace. Even though it was late spring, the nights were cool and a fire still burned. But Momma shivered so badly that I knew it wouldn't be enough.

"Put her in my bed," Abner said. "She'll be warmer there."

We did just that and covered her in a pile of quilts and blankets. I touched her forehead—her sweat felt like icy slush.

Abner pulled pillows and two quilts from his closet and we

made a bed in the corner of the room where we could keep an eye on Momma. I told him everything that had happened.

"It was a trap," he said when I finished.

"Yeah. If we stay in the house when Bishop Stoll visits, he'll see Momma. If we stay out in the daylight, she becomes too weak to hide. And if we try to sneak back, the constables and Vita Dei catch us." And I knew he would return. If not the coming Sunday, then another Sunday. Or another day. He wouldn't give up. Just as I knew Momma wouldn't survive another trip out into the daytime world.

"We need to kill Bishop Stoll," Abner said quietly. "He's behind all this. Probably wants to drag your mother out in front of everyone so they can see one of the monsters he's always talking about."

Something clicked in my chest. A happy clicking, as if my body was saying I'd finally found a true home. I snuggled closer to Abner.

"I won't let you do that," I said. "You killing someone, I mean. But I appreciate the offering."

Abner wrapped his arm around me so his wrist was right before my mouth. I teethed it gently.

We fell asleep at some point. That night I dreamed Momma stood above me smiling, a smile that ran the entire length of her face until she leaned over and her giant mouth kissed me.

But in the morning, she was still asleep in Abner's bed, and I knew it had only been a happy dream.

AFTER RESTING IN ABNER'S BED FOR A FEW DAYS, MOMMA returned to the living room, but instead of taking her spot next to the fireplace, she pulled a chair to the front window overlooking the street and harbor. She sat there with the window and drapes open so the morning sunlight and breeze washed over her.

But this also made it easier for people to see her.

Abner's mother was the first to discover her. She walked into the living room one morning and screamed.

"Hello, Joanie," Momma said. "Don't you remember me?"

"Who ... no, I ..." Abner's mother said. She looked at Abner, who sat next to me at the dining room table eating breakfast. Thankfully, she still couldn't see me.

"Who's that woman by the window?" she asked her son.

"You really want to know? Might be disturbing, like when you caught me in the water closet."

I groaned and walked over to tap Abner's mother on the forehead so she'd forget, but Momma said to stop.

"I'm a ripper," Momma told Joanie. "I killed your husband to stop him from hurting you and your son. I've protected you and this home for many months."

Joanie walked toward her. I felt the memories returning to Joanie's mind of Momma and I killing her husband in the snow. As she remembered, she turned and saw me beside Abner.

I waved.

"This is true?" Joanie asked. "This is all true, isn't it?"

"It is indeed," Abner said.

Momma stood up and walked to the sofa, where she gestured for Joanie to sit beside her.

"You two do your best friend thing somewhere else," Momma told me and Abner. "We mothers need to talk."

❧

IT WAS STRANGE BEING SEEN BY JOANIE. WHILE I DIDN'T hear what she and Momma talked about—even I'm not stupid enough to ignore Momma when she says to leave—whatever they discussed changed everything.

When Joanie and Abner sat at the table to eat dinner, Momma and I joined them. We didn't eat of course, but we talked. Momma described our lives in our old village and some of the Alexanders she'd killed and eaten over the years. She also talked about my older sisters, each of whom had gone out into the world and been killed. And she described how Alexanders had hunted down all of them except for her granddaughter Ziee and myself.

Then she patted me on the head in front of everyone and said that she'd never let Stoll's people kill her last daughter.

Joanie cried, and Abner got misty eyed.

When it was my turn to talk, I mentioned how much I liked reading penny dreadfuls with Abner. My stomach growled while watching Joanie and Abner eat, but Momma waved this away with a promise that we'd be eating again soon.

After that, Momma and Joanie hung around each other as if they'd been best friends their entire lives.

"What the hell are they up to?" Abner asked when he came downstairs to the store one morning before it opened. Momma had told me to shoo, and the store was as far as I could go without actually stepping into the daylight world.

"They kicked you out too?" I asked.

"Yeah. They're whispering about stuff. And my mom hugged your mom."

"Momma didn't bite her?" I didn't need to remind him about Momma's views on hugs.

He shook his head.

I told him to wait in the shop and sneaked back up the stairs.

Our mothers were talking in low voices, standing near the fireplace where Momma and I had slept so many times.

"Amelia told me about you catching Abner in the water closet," Momma said.

I flinched, embarrassed that she'd brought that up. Joanie also blushed.

"Bishop Stoll told me it was unnatural, Abner liking men," Joanie said hesitantly, as if unsure of herself.

"Bishop Stoll thinks I'm unnatural," Momma said. "And when you went to the church to get them to stop your husband from beating you and Abner, the clergy acted as if such abuse was the most natural of things."

Anger boiled out of Joanie at that memory.

"You are very fortunate," Momma said. "Amelia experiences love and other emotions, but, like other rippers, I don't. I would give anything to experience with Amelia the love you have for your son. Don't let some high and mighty man tell you what's natural or unnatural—don't let him break the love you and your son feel."

Joanie hugged Momma again, who froze with her hands out as if still not knowing how to react. Tears slid down my face. I started to tell myself rippers don't cry before deciding to hell with it; there was nothing wrong with crying.

I slipped silently back down the stairs.

"What were they saying?" Abner asked.

I hugged Abner, causing him to freeze for a moment like Momma before he hugged me back.

❧

MOMMA STILL HADN'T RECOVERED FROM BEING FORCED outside all day in the sunshine, so when Saturday night rolled around, I told her I was going hunting for both of us.

She lay on the sofa next to the fireplace. Joanie had declared that Momma wouldn't sleep on the floor in her house and gave her the sofa, even moving it closer to the fire.

"Be safe," she said. "You'd better come back."

I rushed downstairs, only to find Abner waiting at the back door. He wore dark clothes and a black hat pulled low over his head.

"I'm going hunting with you," he announced.

I rolled my eyes but simply said, "Come on."

I figured we'd hunt in the warehouse district. Fairways and Ziee had decided to close the bar because the danger of allowing patrons from across the city to visit was too great. Tonight was the final time the bar would be open, with Fairways hosting a goodbye party for his staff. Hunting near the bar would give us the opportunity to see Fairways, Oscar, and Ziee, and if the hunt got too dangerous I could leave Abner there for a bit.

But as we approached, we discovered hundreds of Vita Dei blocking our way, circling the warehouse district and carrying unlit torches along with pistols and rifles.

"That's not good," Abner said.

I agreed. Leaving him hidden in an alley, I sneaked closer to a group of Vita Dei to see what they were up to. I reached into their minds, trying to not be overwhelmed by the memories of the people they'd hurt. In their squad leader's thoughts, I saw a memory of Bishop Stoll telling the Vita Dei to kill everyone they found in one particular warehouse after dark. They were to circle the district then slowly close in, preventing anyone from escaping. And when they reached the warehouse containing 'the bar for perverts,' as Stoll described it, they were to burn everything to the ground.

"Shit." I rushed back to Abner.

"They're going to burn Fairways' warehouse," I said. "They've circled the entire district so no one can escape."

"We have to warn them," Abner said.

"A warning won't be enough. No one from the bar will be able to escape all these Vita Dei." I paused. "Not without help."

Most of the warehouses in the district were abandoned, which is what made it a great place for Fairways' bar. Normally, people could enter and leave the district from multiple directions, making it easy to slip in and out. But this many Vita Dei could keep people boxed in no matter which way they went. And Abner and I couldn't get in unless we fought our way past them.

I looked at the warehouse wall rising up next to us in the alley.

"You feel like climbing?" I asked. "We can see more from up high."

Abner piggybacked me as I grew my claws. I stabbed them into the bricks and climbed seven stories to the top of the warehouse. From there we could see across the district.

"The Vita Dei are still a few blocks from the bar," Abner said, looking into the distance.

I glared at the advancing vigilantes, my anger at the injustices around me burning stronger than anything I'd ever experienced. Now I understood why anger was the main emotion rippers felt—anger fed into and powered the world within me.

Abner started to say more but then paused. "Err, what's that clicking?"

The anger built up within me as my millions of teeth chittered and clacked, begging to rip apart the violent people trying to kill those I loved.

But where most rippers built their worlds solely from anger, I also felt the other emotions I experienced creating the world inside me. My love for Momma, Abner, Ziee, and everyone else. My sadness at all the people who'd been hurt by Bishop Stoll and the Vita Dei. My happiness at finding a new home in this city. My fear for the safety of my new friends. My hope for a better future for everyone. All these emotions and more built up the world within me into something far stronger than anything created by anger alone.

I felt stronger than ever before. I wasn't going to allow my friends to be hurt. I was going to save them.

"Amelia," Abner said, grabbing my shoulder. "What's wrong?"

I took a deep breath to calm myself. "Nothing's wrong. Do you trust me?"

My best friend nodded.

"Then climb on my back—I'm going to jump to the next warehouse."

Abner looked across the street at the warehouse, and then

down. The roads between warehouses were wide, allowing multiple horse-drawn wagons back in the day to pass side-by-side with room to spare. I scented fear on Abner, but to his credit he climbed onto my back without hesitation.

I glanced at the dark night sky and hoped the Vita Dei weren't looking up. But who looked up when trying to kill people standing before them?

The warehouse roofs were all covered in slate shingles and steeply angled. I needed to build up enough speed to jump without slipping down over the edge.

With Abner holding tight, I climbed to the ridge at the top of the roof, ran forward, and launched myself into the sky. I landed on the edge of the next roof and almost slipped, sending a few slate shingles crashing behind me, but kept running. I picked up speed as the teeth inside me grew more powerful. I wouldn't let Bishop Stoll's plan succeed! I jumped off the roof and landed on the next warehouse with room to spare.

Six more jumps and we reached Fairways' warehouse. To Abner's credit, he didn't scream even once.

We found a rooftop access door that was unlocked and ran downstairs as fast as we could.

When we burst into the bar, Ziee, Fairways, and Oscar were standing with a handful of staff, looking worried.

"How the hell did you get here?" Ziee asked.

"More importantly, why the hell are you here?" Fairways said. "The Vita Dei are only a block away. Now you're trapped with us."

I suddenly realized how silly I was coming here without a plan. I should've known Ziee and Fairways wouldn't be caught off-guard.

"Well, what's your plan?" I asked. "Wait here until they burn the building down?"

"What are you talking about?" he asked.

I told them how Bishop Stoll had ordered the Vita Dei to burn the warehouse down. Ziee cursed.

"We chose this place so we'd be safe if anyone attacked," Fairways said, pointing at the large metal door. "Thick brick walls, massive doors. We'd simply wait out any attackers, then escape later."

"That's no longer a plan I'd go with," I said.

Billy and the bartender Julia walked over to the door, with Julia cracking it open slightly to look outside. A moment later, a gunshot rang out and a bullet zinged off the door. She calmly closed the door and bolted it shut while Billy cursed.

"Amelia's correct," Julia said. "They're carrying buckets of kerosene and lit torches."

More gunshots ripped into the thick walls and bounced off the door.

"I'm going out," Ziee said. "I'll attack them, keep them distracted. While I do that, the rest of you get away."

She headed for the door, but Fairways grabbed her arm. "That's suicide," he shouted.

"Getting killed helps no one," Billy said, with Julia nodding to his words.

But I agreed with Ziee's plan: better to die fighting back than to be burned to death doing nothing. I was telling Ziee I'd go fight alongside her when Abner yelled for everyone to shut up.

"Why can't we go back the same way Amelia and I got here?" he asked.

"Which, of course, was the very question you didn't answer earlier," Ziee said. "How *did* you get here?"

I explained how I'd carried Abner on my back and jumped from rooftop to rooftop.

At first, everyone looked a little stunned, as if I'd said we'd all flap our arms and fly to the moon to escape, or that Ziee would turn into a whale and swim us to safety on her back. Then Billy clapped his giant hands and shouted "Hell yes! This is why I fucking love monsters!" Julia and the two waiters looked a little less enthusiastic, but considering the circumstance said they were also willing to try.

But Ziee looked at me with a puzzled expression.

"Jumping like that takes a lot of energy," she said. "How'd you make it?"

Instead of answering, I clicked the teeth inside me, the sound chattering so loud that for a moment it drowned out the gunshots from outside.

Ziee laid a hand on my shoulder and leaned close to my ear. "I'm proud of you," she whispered. Then louder, she said, "We can do this! It'll take both of us doing multiple trips, but it's the best plan we've got."

"Three of us," Fairways said. "I am a vampire after all. I can jump farther than either of you."

Ziee rolled her eyes. "Fine. The three of us."

There was a splashing sound—liquid being thrown against the walls—and the scent of kerosene as it flowed under the large door.

"Everyone, up the stairs," Abner shouted, grabbing Oscar's hand and dragging his friend after him. Billy pushed the rest of the staff toward the stairs.

Fairways smiled at me. "I'm glad I saved your life, young lady," he said.

"I seem to remember you were actually trying to save Ziee's life," I pointed out.

"Minor detail. What matters is that you're here with us today."

"Be emotional later," Ziee said, shoving us toward the stairs.

We made it to the stairway just as the bar erupted in flames.

We ran up several flights of stairs and exited through the access door onto the rooftop.

"How long until the flames reach us?" Abner asked.

I had no idea. I walked to the edge of the roof and glanced down at the Vita Dei. The vigilantes were still shooting at the warehouse walls, with ricochets hitting several of their own. Their leaders yelled at them to save their ammo for anyone fleeing the building, but the fools kept firing.

Ziee pointed into the distance. "We'll go to that warehouse on the edge of the district. According to Amelia, the Vita Dei aren't over there. We'll jump from here to the next warehouse roof, leave whoever we're carrying, and come back for everyone else. We'll repeat that over and over, warehouse to warehouse, until we're safe."

Fairways gestured for Oscar to get on his back, but his son shook his head. "I'll go last," Oscar said. "Save everyone else first."

"Yeah, I don't want to hear Billy bellyaching if he's left behind," said Julia.

"I'll stay back too," Abner said.

My heart jumped. If the flames climbed too fast, my best friend would die. But I was also impressed by his bravery.

Abner, Oscar and Julia sheltered near the ridge running down the middle of the roof.

"Hop on," I told one of the waiters.

Ziee took the other waiter, while Fairways told Billy to climb on his back.

"You'll notice Billy is six foot eight and three hundred pounds of muscle," Fairways told Ziee. "Of course I'm the only one who can carry him and save his ass."

"Please," she said. "I've already saved Billy's ass twice during his lifetime."

Billy looked at me and sighed, as if wishing he'd chosen a different monster to ride. "Mister Douglas, Miss Ziee," he said, "would you two mind saving us first and bickering later?"

We could already feel the fire's heat coming up through the slate shingles. I told the waiter on my back not to scream as I ran across the roof and jumped to the next warehouse.

Ziee followed behind me, although she didn't run as fast and couldn't jump as far as I did. Fairways turned out to be a powerhouse at jumping, outdistancing both of us.

Once we reached the far side of the next warehouse's roof, we hid Billy and the others beside a chimney. We then raced back for Abner, Oscar and Julia. As we jumped, I saw flames already erupting near the warehouse roof where Abner, Oscar, and Julia waited.

As I landed on the burning warehouse, flames singed my clothes. Shingles cracked and smashed underneath me as I ran to safety, the roof already sagging dangerously. The flames were spreading so fast that by the time we reached Abner,

Oscar, and Julia, we couldn't run back the same way we'd come.

I pointed toward an unburned area of brickwork along the edge of the roof. "Run that way and launch yourself off the parapet," I yelled to Fairways and Ziee. "It should still be sturdy."

Fairways picked up Oscar and ran, launching himself across the gap to the next warehouse. Ziee followed with Julia on her back. Abner climbed on my back as I waited for Ziee to get clear.

"You can do this," Abner said.

I grinned as the building under us creaked ominously. The portion of the roof to my right shuddered as if the warehouse was breathing but I ignored it, running across the slate shingles and launching myself from the parapet. I touched down on the roof of the next warehouse but landed wrong, Abner and I sliding across the slates until Fairways grabbed us, stopping our tumble.

"Wow," Abner said as we looked back at the warehouse we'd jumped from. We watched the entire roof we'd stood on just moments before collapsing in a cloud of glowing sparks and embers.

"We need to keep moving," Ziee ordered.

We kept ferrying the others from roof to roof until we reached an area outside the Vita Dei's trap. The flames from the fire that had fully engulfed the warehouse with Fairways' bar were now spread to the other nearby buildings. But that was the Vita Dei's problem now, not ours.

"I'll give you two credits for one thing," Billy said, pulling Fairways and Ziee into a massive hug. "You throw a hell of a going away party."

ABNER AND I WALKED HOME IN THE DARK WITH ZIEE, WHO we'd offered a place to stay. The others had dispersed to their homes, and Fairways and Oscar had gone to a close friend's house. That left only Ziee needing a place to stay. While she was stronger than Momma, being out in the daylight would still drain her energy. Especially with so many Alexanders patrolling the streets.

Ziee was uncomfortable about coming home with us, but she couldn't stay with Fairways' friend without questions being asked.

"My mom absolutely won't mind," Abner said. "I mean, you and Amelia saved my life."

"You going to tell your mother that Amelia endangered your life in the first place by allowing you to join her hunt?" Ziee asked.

I was pretty sure she was joking, but I still sighed.

"Anyway, Abner's right—stay with us," I said. "I'll make sure Momma is okay with it. After all, what kind of aunt would I be if I didn't look after my niece?"

Ziee glared at me, her eyebrows smoking as twin flames popped up on her cheeks. "What did you say?" she said in menacing voice.

"It's okay," I joked. "I won't make you call me Auntie Amelia all the time."

WE MADE IT HOME JUST BEFORE DAYLIGHT, THE MORNING sun rising not long after we sat down at the dining room table and told Momma and Joanie what had happened. Out the window we watched the smoke haze from the burning warehouses float over the harbor. The sunlight mixed with the smoke tinted the boats and ships tied up at the docks in a faint red color.

Momma and Joanie were indeed okay with Ziee staying in the house. However, despite all of us feeling exhausted from being up all night and barely escaping with our lives, Momma said we should stay awake.

"It's Sunday," she pointed out. "The Bishop may try to stir up trouble at the cathedral today, and the Vita Dei will definitely be emboldened by last night's attack. We need to keep watch in case of trouble."

Joanie agreed with Momma. She also told Abner he didn't need to come to church.

"I'm going to pop over to the cathedral one last time," she added. "Need to tell some friends that I won't be coming back to services after today."

Once Joanie was gone, Abner and I went downstairs to the store. A new delivery of penny dreadfuls had arrived the other day, which Joanie had hidden behind the counter so no one could see. Even if it wasn't safe to sell the booklets, we could absolutely read them ourselves.

I was so engrossed in a vampire story that I didn't notice Momma and Ziee standing before me until Momma spoke.

"I don't understand what you two see in those stories," Momma said.

I thought she was just making idle conversation, but then she walked to the store's big picture window. Though her body was still weak, she seemed more focused than she'd been in months, and almost eager.

People coming back from church walked by the front window, with the smoky sunlight illuminating her. Despite that, Momma stood where anyone looking in could see her.

"You'll be seen," I stammered. I ran to her and grabbed her arm to drag her from the window. But she was stronger than she looked and wouldn't be moved.

"I want them to see," Momma said. "Joanie is bringing Bishop Stoll and the Vita Dei. And I'm going to remind this city why rippers exist."

I glared at Abner, thinking his mother had betrayed us, but his face showed he was as surprised as I was.

"I asked Joanie to do this," Momma said. "At most I'll live another year. But if the city keeps going as it is, none of you will survive that long. I want to change that."

"I'll fight with you," I said.

"Me too," said Ziee.

"If you two do that, all this will be a waste. And they'll know Joanie was lying when she told them there was only one monster here. They'll come after her and Abner."

I started to argue but suddenly tasted Alexanders approaching. A very large number of Alexanders. Momma growled and pushed us back from the window as Joanie, Bishop Stoll, and Constable Rasner approached, followed by three dozen Vita Dei, including Belker.

"Hide yourselves," Momma told me and Ziee.

"But I can help ..." I stammered.

"Grandmother, please," Ziee said in a low voice.

The Vita Dei waited in the street while Joanie, Bishop Stoll, and Constable Rasner walked to the front door. Stoll waved impatiently for Joanie to unlock it.

"Hide yourselves," Momma told me and Ziee. "This is what a mother does."

Momma patted us both on the head before striding toward the opening door.

Joanie was the first through the door, followed by Bishop Stoll and Constable Rasner.

"If you'd been paying attention," Constable Rasner said, chastising Joanie instead of looking around the store, "you'd have known before today that a monster killed your husband."

Joanie ran out of the way as Momma walked up to Constable Rasner. She created a blood-maw and used it to bite off the constable's head and upper body—the easiest kill I'd ever seen her make.

Bishop Stoll stared at Momma in shock. The Vita Dei outside also stared at the bloody scene through the store's large picture window. I imagine they'd expected to fight a monster as she fled outside, not be forced to charge inside at one who'd just decapitated a constable. They looked to their squad leader Belker as if asking him what to do, but Belker was too shocked to respond.

"You can't escape," Bishop Stoll stammered.

"I still have time to kill you," Momma said. Eating a third of Constable Rasner had given her more energy than she'd had in days. But as she stepped toward Stoll, bright orange flames rippled across her face and arms.

"Ahh, we know you can't do that," the bishop said. "Rippers only kill those who do violence to others, such as our dear departed Constable Rasner. I've never hurt a soul."

"You created the Vita Dei. You've ordered them to kill and torture people across the city."

"But I've never personally hurt anyone."

She took another step toward him, but her magic burned her even brighter—if she continued, she'd quickly lose the energy she'd gained from eating Constable Rasner.

With a yell, she ran outside into the daylight. The other Vita Dei had finally overcome their shock, and Belker was urging them to rush the door and save Bishop Stoll. But where Momma couldn't hurt Stoll, these Vita Dei were Alexanders like Rasner.

Claws emerged from Momma's fingers and she sliced open the stomach of one Vita Dei and severed the right arm of a second. The men screamed while the other vigilantes jumped back in fear. Controlling her blood-maw like a puppet, Momma whipped it toward two Vita Dei, dragging them into her hell.

But it wasn't merely Momma and the Vita Dei outside. People walking home from church or on their way to work on the fishing trawlers and sailing ships in the bay were also passing by. Now they stared at Momma. Her blood-maw swirled before her with visions of hell. Her teeth chattered loudly against one another like a million drums banging across the waterfront.

Everyone saw Momma for what she was: a ripper.

She stabbed her claws into the chest of an Alexander aiming a pistol at her. Bishop Stoll, nearby constables, passing church goers, fishermen and sailors, and every other person in the area gasped as they experienced the man's sins. In addition to being a member of the church's Vita Dei, this Alexander was also a murderer who'd killed a half-dozen people in recent years. He'd imagined himself a hero, ridding the city of those people he considered worthless. But in reality, he merely wanted people to suffer.

I shuddered, as did the other people watching. Momma fed what she tasted into everyone's minds so they could see the pain and violence this Alexander had created.

"My God," Bishop Stoll said. "What a monster."

He was speaking about Momma, not the Alexander who'd killed so many people over the years. I growled in anger.

"Come," Joanie whispered as she grabbed my hand. "Your mother wanted us to hide you until it was safe."

I didn't move, only watched as Momma attacked more of the Vita Dei and continued to share their evil deeds with those around us. She ripped Belker in half while sharing how he'd tortured a woman merely because she worked as both a midwife and an abortionist. I heard another gasp as everyone along the waterfront experienced Belker's memories of the woman pleading for mercy—a mercy he never granted as he stretched her on the rack.

But using so much magic in the daylight was quickly exhausting Momma. One of the Vita Dei fired his revolver, striking her in the leg. Others also fired but missed.

I stepped forward, but Ziee grabbed my arm. "Amelia, you can't save her," she said. "There are too many Alexanders. And like Danjay said, if we reveal ourselves, they'll hurt Joanie and Abner."

"I know. But I can do something."

I kissed Ziee on the cheek. I was indeed a strange little monster, so very different from my mother or niece. Or any other ripper that ever existed.

I walked toward Bishop Stoll and the remains of Constable Rasner's body, which had bled all over the wood floor I'd swept so many times with Abner. Momma could have eaten all of Rasner if she'd wanted, which would have given her a little more energy for her final fight. Instead, she'd left part of him for me to eat later, after it was safe. How very motherly of her.

But I wouldn't be eating Rasner.

Bishop Stoll stood before the large store window, watching from safety as Momma fought. He gripped his crucifix with one hand as Momma bit a Vita Dei's shoulder and ripped out a hunk of bone and flesh while also sharing with everyone how that Alexander had helped the constables beat prisoners in the jail.

The wooden floor creaked as I neared Bishop Stoll. He turned and started.

"Who are you?" he asked. He glanced at Joanie and Abner, as if silently asking if I was an unknown daughter and sister. He still couldn't see Ziee, who stood before the window with a horrified look in her eyes as she watched her grandmother die.

I split my face into a massive grin, revealing my fangs. My claws glowed to fire as I swirled them before me and opened a blood-maw, revealing for the first time my own private world of grinding teeth. My face and arms burned as my magic fought against me even thinking of harming this evil man.

"She had a little spawn, did she," Bishop Stoll said. "That explains so much. Well, Miss Monster, you can't hurt me, the same as your mother."

"I'm not the same as my mother," I said, stepping forward. "I can love. I can cry. I can do things Momma only dreamed of."

As I reached for Bishop Stoll, I saw his sins. He'd counselled so many women over the years to stay with abusive men, merely because their marriages had been declared sacred by the church. He'd turned people like Abner over to the authorities for punishment, merely because those in power deemed their love unnatural. He'd created the Vita Dei to hunt not only monsters like me but also anyone who disagreed with him.

And I saw him hunting down my Momma, no cares about the justice Momma brought to people who otherwise received none. I saw all the Alexanders he'd not only allowed to live but actively helped so they could hurt people who didn't agree with Stoll's view of the world. And I saw the massive pain inflicted by arrogant and powerful men like him across the centuries, harming far more people than the individual Alexanders we already hunted.

He was an Alexander. Not like the other Alexanders, but still an Alexander. Just as I wasn't a ripper like Momma and Ziee, but still a ripper.

I laughed as my magic stopped burning my skin.

"Impossible," Bishop Stoll said.

He tried to run but my blood-maw swallowed him whole, row after row of my teeth tearing and chewing his body before he could even scream. I swallowed his sins and swallowed his hate and swallowed his anger and swallowed his fears.

I swallowed it all, so he'd never again hurt anyone in this world.

"How the hell did you do that?" Ziee asked, shocked.

I merely shook my head and looked out the window.

Momma was still fighting the Vita Dei, but she was so injured that she could barely move. As her claws sliced a Vita

Dei across the face, she looked in through the store window at me. She'd tasted Bishop Stoll's sins as I'd eaten him. She knew that I'd been able to see him as an Alexander when she couldn't.

One of the Vita Dei raised a pistol toward Momma's head, but she didn't dodge or turn. Instead, she kept looking at me and smiled the first true smile I'd ever seen on her face.

Instead of screaming when she died, Ziee and I followed Abner and Joanie upstairs, where they hid us while I cried.

Ziee sat next to me and patted my head. I noticed a tear roll down her face, but I didn't say anything because she still believed rippers shouldn't cry.

❦

TWO MONTHS LATER, ABNER AND I SAT BEHIND THE STORE counter reading penny dreadfuls on a slow Saturday afternoon.

Outside, several kids peeked in the window, trying to see the blood stains left by Bishop Stoll and Constable Rasner. While Abner and I had spent days scrubbing the floor, there was still a large dark stain near the front door.

The kids pointed and squealed. I rolled my eyes even as I reached into their minds to make sure they couldn't see me.

"They'd have really squealed if they'd had to clean that shit up," Abner said.

I laughed. So many constables and city officials and priests had come by after Momma's fight that we hadn't gotten a chance to clean the floor for a good while. By the time we did, the blood had congealed to a hard, sticky mess that even I found disgusting.

In the end, no one discovered me or Ziee. We'd reached into the minds of the Vita Dei who'd survived and convinced them that Momma had also eaten Bishop Stoll before she attacked everyone outside.

"We might as well close up for the night," I said, hopping from my seat. I locked the front door, taking a moment to stare at the melted votive candles across the street.

The city had been in an uproar when Momma was killed. The city leaders, all fine men of unimpeachable character, declared that monsters like my mother couldn't be tolerated. The priests thundered from their pulpits, proclaiming Bishop Stoll a martyr and saint. The Vita Dei promised even more patrols.

But the people along the waterfront who'd witnessed the fight knew the truth. Thanks to Momma, they'd realized how many people the Vita Dei had hurt. Several times a week, people now lit candles on the stone pier across from the store. Always at night. Always when the priests, Vita Dei, and constables weren't looking.

I made sure to reach out to them as they lit their candles. I listened to their prayers for deliverance from abusive husbands and partners and parents, or for protection from the constables and the Vita Dei.

And most surprising, once an Alexander even stopped and lit a candle, apologizing for what he'd done and promising to do better.

"You going hunting tonight?" Abner asked as he walked up behind me.

"Yeah. The woman who lit the candle last night needs help."

Abner hugged me.

As word spread about the evil being committed by the Vita Dei, more and more people were standing up to them. People in the waterfront district—lead by Billy and Julia—had been the first to force the Vita Dei to end their patrols here. Now it sounded like other neighborhoods were trying to do the same.

So far, Fairways, Oscar, and Ziee were safe in their new midtown home, which they'd purchased not long after their bar burned down. Fairways told me they were already looking for a place to build their next bar once the city calmed down a bit more. And Ziee stopped by the shophouse every week or so—always in the evenings, of course. While she still refused to call me Auntie Amelia, we now hunted together. Our targets were the powerful Alexanders in charge of the Vita Dei, the incendiaries in the church, and the city officials who enabled them.

Ziee once asked me to teach her how to kill incendiaries, but when I told her the first step was to let more emotions into her life, she hesitated and said she'd have to think about that.

LATER THAT YEAR ABNER AND I SAT READING PENNY dreadfuls in the store when we heard Joanie calling us to dinner—or more accurately, calling Abner to eat and me to watch. But it was still nice to sit at the table and feel a family's love.

Abner started towards the stairs, but I grabbed his hand, stopping him.

"Um, I never asked," I said, struggling to get the words

out. "I mean, you saw me kill the bishop. You saw what I am. Does that bother you?"

Abner smiled and squeezed my hand. "Yes, I saw what you are. And I love who you are."

I remembered Momma's words when she caught me and Abner sleeping side by side. That I was a ripper. That I couldn't do the physical things humans did when they were in love. I also knew that Abner still liked men. Eventually he'd find a human who'd accept him for who he was, and who could do the things humans did with each other when they were in love.

The love I felt for Abner was different from all that. But what exactly was our love?

"But as Momma said, I'm not human. You know what I am. You're really okay with that?"

"Why wouldn't I be okay with you?"

"Because in all those stories we read, people love each other for one of two reasons: They are family, or they want to mate. Our love doesn't fit either of those. I don't understand it."

Abner smirked, then he laughed. I frowned, which caused him to try and stop laughing. But that only made him laugh even harder.

"Wait, wait," he said, catching his breath. "I'm not laughing at what you said. I'm laughing at who said it."

"What?" I said, starting to grow angry.

Abner grabbed my shoulders, holding me before him. "You're the ripper like no other ripper. You have emotions no other ripper has ever experienced. You killed an Alexander other rippers couldn't touch. That's why I'm laughing—you've already done so many things you weren't supposed to do.

Why can't our love be like that? Maybe it's different from any other love that ever existed."

I thought about that. Different. I could accept that.

"I still don't know what will happen with us."

"Same. Guess we'll have to find our own path. But the good news is that we'll figure it out together."

He kissed me on the cheek before going upstairs.

I waited in the empty store as my eyes teared up. I no longer believed that rippers didn't experience love or sadness or any of the other emotions I felt. Because I was a ripper and I knew all those things.

I'd accepted that I'll never be like the other rippers, just as Abner now accepted that he'd never be what Bishop Stoll and the church falsely claimed men should be.

We'd always be different, and so would our love and friendship.

For now, that would be good enough.

END

ABOUT THE AUTHOR

Jason Sanford is an award-winning science fiction and fantasy writer who's also a passionate advocate for fellow authors, creators, and fans, in particular through reporting in his Genre Grapevine column (for which he's been a finalist multiple times for the Hugo Award for Best Fan Writer). He's also published dozens of stories in magazines such as *Asimov's Science Fiction, Apex Magazine, Interzone,* and *Beneath Ceaseless Skies* along with appearances in various "year's best" anthologies and *The New Voices of Science Fiction.* His first novel *Plague Birds* was a finalist for both the 2022 Nebula Award and the 2022 Philip K. Dick Award. Born and raised in the American South, Jason's previous experience includes work as an archaeologist, journalist and a Peace Corps Volunteer. His website is www.jasonsanford.com.

ACKNOWLEDGMENTS

Thank you to everyone who attended the inaugural PubQ Writing Retreat for the inspiration, motivation and friendships that made this novella possible. Thanks also to my agent Lucienne Diver for supporting this strange little story and to Jason Sizemore and Darian Bianco of Apex Books for giving *We Who Hunt Alexanders* such a wonderful, loving home. Finally, special thanks to Marissa van Uden for the amazing copy editing.

"An action-packed and riveting page-turner…"
—Mercurio D. Rivera, World Fantasy Award-nominated author
PLAGUE BIRDS
JASON SANFORD

www.ingramcontent.com/pod-product-compliance
Lightning Source LLC
Chambersburg PA
CBHW021717190726
48289CB00008B/2580